Market Day

THE HUNGARIAN LIST

Market Day

PÁL ZÁVADA

Translated by
OWEN GOOD

LONDON NEW YORK CALCUTTA

Seagull Books, 2023

First published in Hungarian as *Egy piaci nap* by Pál Závada
© Pál Závada, 2016

English translation rights arranged with Magvető Publishing, Budapest

First published in English translation by Seagull Books, 2023
English translation © Owen Good, 2023

ISBN 978 1 8030 9 160 0

British Library Cataloguing-in-Publication Data
A catalogue record for this book is available from the British Library

Typeset at Seagull Books, Calcutta, India
Printed and bound Hyam Enterprises, Calcutta, India

Market Day

I can say the exact moment it hit me that amid this tempest, we would be the ones struck by the biggest bolt of them all. That covering my eyes in horror no longer offered any protection. That I could run home and shove my head under the pillow because I abhorred what these people were doing—but it would be no use. Because not only were others threatened before our very eyes by this onslaught, but we too would be fixed as targets and stormed, this became clear that very minute.

More precisely, on Görbe Street behind the market, when in full view of the dispersing but still angry mob, the other half of the tall wooden gate swings open, and an unfamiliar policeman and a civilian appear, carrying an unconscious body under the arms and legs, while I watch. And not right away—you can't help but be drawn to the bloody gash in the crotch showing through the torn trousers, while the only part unharmed on the battered head and face is the goatee—but regaining my senses from the shock and looking more closely at the victim, I recognize Ferenc Gross the egg seller. Whose gate I am standing in front of. A small lorry pulls up, out jumps an officer—if you'll just forgive us, madam, ushering me aside with surprising refinement—so as then he and two others can lift the injured onto the empty flatbed and drive off.

God Almighty it's awful, I whisper, poor Ferenc will hardly survive and after that there will be a whole new chapter. Because if people start calling for someone to blame, mark my words, we will be singled out first.

I walked back to the main street, now emptying and glittered with glass from broken windows, and I headed for my childhood home. I knew that my father had learnt from when the Russians had ploughed through here a year and a half back, so I would find his haberdashers and fashion store unharmed—unlike the ransacked shops and trampled market stalls—both his displays were protected with indestructible steel shutters, likewise at the house he had drawn the shutters on all six windows and locked the gate. But I didn't want to drop in, nor did I take the back street where I could have woken Julcsa, our old maid, with a knock on the window of her house—I wasn't in the mood to hear my father's opinion on the situation in the streets, or his advice, which no doubt he would air, though I was the one who had been there and not him.

And when I got home, I didn't feel like saying a word of it to my husband either—perhaps because of my unspeakable dread that he might be at threat from what was raging outdoors, though not for any fault of his own. I lied to him, said I didn't go to the square, I heard the shouting and yelling, apparently a few rowdy types chased off the sellers and knocked their crates over. But I only had a word with Julcsa through the window, I say to him, my parents have the doors locked, they've no need for anything, and I saw nothing out of the ordinary on the back street when I ran to theirs. So not only did I keep quiet to him about what was actually going on outside, but also that poor Ferenc Gross, beaten to death, had just been carried out before my eyes, and the sheer terror that took over me.

Sándor didn't notice that what I had rattled off to him could only account for at most thirty minutes, not an hour and a half. But still I saw that even my quite filtered news had made him nervous, he expressed his own wondering as to how far the upheaval might go, and whether or not the police could bring order soon enough, but persuaded himself to stay calm. He went on pouring cups of tepid, bland tea substitute from the enamel jug, and from a thick textbook made an abstract of the various cereal pests, writing in a blue-lined notebook in his pearly letters. He didn't so much as raise an eyebrow when I said I was going to lie down a spell. All right, Marika dear, go on ahead, and was already thumbing through his book in search of something.

*

I drew the shutters, lay down to rest, and started thinking about the morning of the day before, the anxious excitement as we set off from home. But never could we have imagined all the things that were to come, and so this fear neither.

No, in fact, as we stood there and a good number of supporters gathered in the mid-morning sun, a pinch of optimism took the edge off my unease, supposing things turned out for the better. On that day, 20th May '46, we met the Smallholders of Kunvadas, our small town, in front of their hall so we could all escort teacher Sándor Hadnagy—my husband—to the People's Court hearing in Karcag. To show our respect for a man who didn't have a dishonest bone in his body, as Sándor's supporters put it themselves, and that's the truth of what they felt, with no exaggeration. Because when it came down to it, an accusation—quickly torn to shreds as

5

hackneyed, incoherent hearsay, no less—had been brought against their children's teacher. That Sándor had, back then, supposedly 'circulated war propaganda' at the market.

What's a man supposed to make of that? Is that really the only reason he was reported?!, grumbled his sympathizers who had gathered for his sake.

And then a day-labourer type in patched trousers broke from his group loitering on the pavement opposite, stepped towards us and jeered:

Oh and what if it isn't? What if there really are more charges against the teacher?

Then he looked round to the three or four more of his ilk, coming abreast of him, speaking over the top of one another, starting provocations as if on cue. Saying, why the long faces on the teacher's reactionary cronies, teasing, has something upset the Littleholders? Then they dubbed our friends whitewashers and bragged about being against us, about joining the local Communist youth. Have we heard of the Hungarian Democratic Youth Association? They are members, they said. And more than willing to explain the accusation against Mr Hadnagy. If we'd like to know, it's that in September '44, when the front was approaching, he armed the cadets under his leadership and took off with them.

So I could save them, called out my husband, Mr Hadnagy himself, wearing a suit and hat with a neat little moustache. I was standing directly behind him.

My eye! That wasn't the reason!, he was immediately drowned out.

That's the truth!, threw back my husband, Boys like those were easy prey, they'd have fallen into the Russians' snare, then next stop Siberia!

That's a lie! You hauled off those teenagers to fight against the Russians! Reactionary! Don't talk rubbish!, shouted the Democratic Youth day labourers, flaunting their leftist consciousness with all sorts of childish boasts; meanwhile they really quite stank.

You ordered them to the defence line, Sándor, don't you deny it!, yelled one tatty swine, using my husband's name.

So Sándor pulled out his silver cigarette case from his inside pocket, popped it open and slipped one into his cigarette holder. Communist traitors—he positioned the holder between his teeth and hissed—would do well to keep their mouths shut!

What's that?, they retaliated in chorus, while he snapped open his petrol lighter and coolly lit up. Shame on you! Running your dirty mouth! Leading children into a hail of bullets . . . !

Not a single hair was touched on their heads, Sándor retorted, sending up clouds of smoke. I brought all sixteen back from the west, safe and sound.

Hear, hear, he's right, our Smallholder friends began to chime in, to the front of whom stood my husband's good friend, Gergely Kátai. Who was in fact the leader of this delegation marching to the court hearing, but seemingly not wanting to delay, he didn't join in, just looked about with a quick, cold smile. People were already readying themselves to set off, those passing around flat bottles of stiff pálinka replaced the cork, while several started backing Sándor.

That the Russians would have rounded those boys up right away to build the airstrip here or sent them packing to the Urals direct. So cut the crap, they threw back at the objectors, our teacher is a hero, safely leading every last one home. Which is why us people who actually matter are here today to defend Mr Hadnagy.

And because he's an honourable man. And good Magyar, good teacher.

He teaches Hungarian?

No. Geography–Biology.

But he was convicted in the first instance, someone argued though everyone in this circle knew; after all, this was precisely why they had gathered, because the trial had been reopened. And because of that shameful judgement brought in June of '45, the one that caused such an uproar all around these parts that it eventually had to be revoked. Everyone knew the hastily botched-together People's Courts were playing from the Communists' notes, and their sentences hadn't the slightest thing to do with justice.

Because false witnesses testified against you, Sándor!

Well of course, the Social Democrats, several nodded. While others exchanged glances and a few added clarifications.

Not even, some weren't Social Dems, they were the ones who came back, from the whatevers.

What? Where?

Who?

Who'd you think?

Oh, you mean . . .

The People's Courts are full of them, to the last man, you understand . . . ?

Of course. And reported him too, in the first place.

Hurts their eyes to see a good Magyar.

Well, answer me this!, the man in patched trousers approached our Smallholders again. Is a man who arms his own teenage pupils to take them into battle honestly a good man in your eyes?

Not to mention on which side!, the rest of the young Communists were getting fired up too. On the fascists' side, against the liberators! That's why he was sentenced to four and a half years, but was let go.

I was standing between the two arguing gangs, and feeling nauseous. I suddenly realized what nauseated me most: the piercing, choking stench. And a different stink from each side—onion and body stink from the finest of the tramps on the left, with pálinka and garlic stink from our sympathetic fellows on the right.

All right, said my husband in a raised voice, just to be clear: the sentence brought against me was reversed by the National Council of the People's Courts. Lawfully. Is that clear to everyone?

But only on the pretext, continued the scruffs, that the National Peasant Party wasn't present at the judicial council! Not due to any absence of a crime, but because of a formality. And right away with a new date for the hearing.

At this point I felt it was time for me to speak up. My husband is innocent, everyone knows that, I stepped forward suddenly—they had barely noticed me until now. He has it on paper. A whole year has gone by, I explained, breathing through my mouth. It was not right away, but a full year later, when Mr Hadnagy was finally summoned for the second instance. That's why we decided we would turn to the parties. While I myself talked to the local Women's Democratic Association. And truly, it worked, one after the other, parties wrote submissions to the People's Court that my husband's case be judged favourably. Except for the Social Democrats—who didn't. Sándor thinks it's no surprise; Károly Würczel is both secretary of the local Social Democrats, and he is also indisputably a . . . well, whatever. Anyway, that's not the point of the matter, the point is that in my husband's legal case, that particular man is one of the prosecutor's witnesses. Well of course he didn't sign.

And seemingly wanting to close proceedings on this time-consuming exchange, Gergely Kátai announces, as though it were a piece of good news: And we all know who the two principal witnesses were, don't we? Communist Party Secretary Ferenc Hámos and his wife, Irén Hámos. Needless to say, they didn't sign either. But let's go, we don't want to miss the hearing.

*

But I want to add a few more words about this altercation in front of the Smallholders' hall.

Now, the accusation fabricated against my Sándor—that he spread war propaganda—originates from events nearly two years ago. Mind you, in May of '44, I would concede it wasn't particularly smart to proclaim on the main square of the village, under the war memorial, to a whole squad of boy cadets that the military situation would be totally flipped on its head by Germany's rockets, her renowned Wonder Weapons, and that we must do everything in our power to thwart the Russian Bolshevik horde, to reclaim our sacred kingdom's thousand-year-old borders.

I agree, Sándor, I said when we argued about it, there is no question, I want the same, I think it would be great. I just don't understand, how you can still believe, that it's actually plausible, that it truly could still happen.

But why on earth would I want to shake his uncompromising loyalty, to something that's a serious question of conscience for him, a question of honour and ultimate faith.

Fine, look, far as I'm concerned you can be as uncompromising as you like, but just, can you do it quietly . . .

How can you say that, Marika? Quietly? To stand in front of my young soldiers, my bravest pupils, and instil morale in them without opening my mouth? To not tell them where to and what for?

Well, if you know the likes of that, Sándor . . . Still, speak about those sorts of things among yourselves, rather than cause a commotion on the main street!

At which he became so hopelessly upset he almost started crying, and repeated that these boys love him more than their own fathers and would blindly follow him anywhere, you know, after all that, how could I talk about such matters with such a cynical and shallow mindset?

And then of course it was no use reminding Sándor about something he seemed to have erased from his memory: that a couple of months ago he had quarrelled with his best friend, too, over this same question. Gergely Kátai had been sent home from the front with an injury, and in spite of his previous zeal as a member of the Hungarian Revival Party, he was completely disappointed, he expected no good outcome. During a powerful drinking session, he revealed his new thinking to Sándor, who upon hearing such defeatism couldn't believe his ears, and afterwards told me, he put it down to Gergely's drunkenness and would hear no more of it. Whereas I advised the contrary, that when it came to judging the military situation (and notions of allegiance and brotherhood-in-arms bordering on doglike stupidity, I added in my head) he might do well to listen to Gergely who's better informed in such matters.

Any time I discussed politics with my husband, I had good reason not to refer to my father's arguments either. My father was always considered an indisputable authority in the village, that is, everyone thought—and after the war our family quietly tried to keep up this appearance—in our small town, that Ignác Csóka, the textile merchant was the singular true Hungarian citizen, prepared for anything, not only because he was always shrewdly calculating and kept useful relations, but also because he was cautiously circumspect and less trustful when it came to human character and virtues. Perhaps as a result, quite soon and to his own irritation, he noticed my husband's close-mindedness in certain political questions. During the last stretch of the war, my father spoke quite offhand about his son-in-law, his opinion being that, given the circumstances, an honourable Hungarian would convert their former pro-German sentiments to pro-English ones. He had breathed a sigh of relief after the Germans' hasty desertion and curtly said he hoped the Russians would leave us in peace. Such a stance was far from my husband's, who would have considered it treasonous.

Now, look what happened? I tried to urge Sándor to be careful, and I was right. That's the exact reason he was reported after the front had passed. That he believed in the Wonder Weapons and in holding back the Bolshevik horde. But was he the only believer? And is it so outlandish of me to suspect that the person who reported him was a person who would also bear false witness against him? That is, it was clear as rain to everyone that Würczel was the person in question. Or Hámos—but probably both.

Initially, I was very understanding of my Sándor's position as a commander of the military youth league, the Levente Movement, later of course I reviled it for leading all their lives into danger. I had always felt his strong, prudent male desire to be a father figure, though he never spoke of it, even to me, and when he told me he had agreed to lead the school Levente brigade, I nodded in approval as if it were to be expected. Yet it wasn't, he hadn't discussed it with me, and though surprised, I accepted right away, without protest. Secretly, it put me at more ease (of which I was ashamed), because it wouldn't be my lot alone to fulfil Sándor's desires.

Because it's true, in the last ten years he hasn't said it out loud, but my husband always had a strong longing for a son or two. They might have been seven or eight by then if I had managed to keep my first pregnancy, but sadly I had a number of issues in that way—and in related ways—which I wouldn't like to get into now. With great difficulty I managed to give birth to a girl with a weak heart, and just as the Lord gave her to us, to find joy in that beautiful, kind, intelligent child, in the autumn of '42, when we would have sent her to school, He took her away. I won't say it was unexpected, the professor in Debrecen said the catastrophe could have come earlier, but the loss of our little Margita hit us so hard that we weren't able to get back on our feet in the years since. Never mind to try again.

We had been childless barely six months when my Sándor, perhaps envious that some of his teaching colleagues met their finest students in study groups and societies, set his sights on taking up office as the Levente Movement commander. Which he believed offered the most various connections between student and teacher, after all, think of all it covers, Marika, sweetheart, he repeated to me, the point is it's not just about intellectual cultivation but the training of the body too, it's more than simply a form of leisurely, useful recreation, it's the practice of doing one's duty. All of this tied in with different kinds of sporting contests or regular war games and military drills. Moreover, in the Levente family, it's not just our fellow men and leaders to whom we pay love and respect, but to our country, first and foremost, and to our own suffering Hungarian Reformed faith. And when it comes to my teenage boys, and myself too, neither the physics study group nor the literature group can offer all this in one package, explained Sándor, the same goes for any sports club or choir.

Over the years I knew little about what they did, my husband didn't talk about it much. I rarely saw them, besides on national holidays in military formation, wearing feathered field caps, heads twisted to the right, parading along the Karcag Road—with my own Sándor at the front, kitted out in boots and straps, marching the goose-step so eagerly I found it comical, but of course never dared say.

I knew even less about the mustering of his cadets in the autumn of '44 and its appointment towards the home front, which later brought trouble. Sándor wasn't willing to talk about the operation—citing military secrets, oh of course!, I say, why would you tell me?, but didn't want to argue—especially afterwards. I'm not even to try asking, there's nothing he can tell me anyway, about where they were, or what they took part in. And none of the boys will talk either, I might as well let the parents know their boys are bound to secrecy. And their oaths will not be forgotten, he would stake his life on it, he knows every one of them, and though he is no longer their teacher, he does everything he can to look out for them, because he has taken each of their sixteen fates to heart.

He only asks that I understand, he explained before their departure: Where he orders his Levente brigade and on what purpose was never his decision alone, and still isn't. But during these pivotal days, it's crucial their actions are coordinated the whole way down the line, which is why everyone owes their strict discipline, their moral loyalty and their allegiance to their superior. Nor can he say who his superior is, but I can be sure if there's a call to assemble, to march out and show their allegiance, it won't be one person's hasty decision but a considered command. And if we're separated by his commitment, I should have absolute faith in their fortune of war, and in him, my wedded husband, who would hold his faith with duty and with honour, and would go through fire and water for the boys entrusted to him.

What could I possibly cling to during those two long days they were gone, if not these outwardly honest, if clichéd, promises? Meanwhile, thinking he might well have faith, but should circumstances force him to his knees, there was little he could do. And what was I to do if he weren't to come home, were injured, were taken prisoner? And what was I to say to the parents if one of their children got into trouble?

The front's passing was brutal because, due to the airfield, our village signified a priority military base. The German troops had started building the airstrip in '43, and even though it was still used then for grazing cattle and sheep, and was only a narrow grass strip, it was well used. To secure their retreat, the Germans deployed their 13th panzer division here and seized school rooms and the empty homes of the deported to lodge more than five hundred soldiers. And of course they heavily defended the airstrip, which the Russians wanted to get their hands on. Which is why we had to endure ghastly bombardments and fierce battles, and unsurprisingly twenty civilians of Kunvadas town had fallen victim by the time the Russians occupied the village and the airstrip, and had started building the crossing over the River Tisza.

Of course, some people say that compared with other theatres of war, this couple of weeks, as the German-Hungarian corps made a hurried retreat through our area, deserting their positions at the first Russian push after a failed attempt to outflank them, was a minor skirmish. But as for what the Russians did in our village and in the area afterwards: to claim there's nothing there worth raking up, compared with what might be called typical stories of murderous bloody pillaging—well, it's better I not comment on such a cynical, insensitive outlook. And I'll say no more on the subject.

It's enough that from our Russian occupation onwards, we passed the time nervously waiting. Me just waiting for my husband, I didn't care whether or not he was welcome, just that he came back unhurt, and I wasn't interested in which of the old guard had fled and which had stayed, despite maybe being better off setting up in some unknown place, or conversely which had the gall to forget their past and, in the new, local National Committee, embrace the hitherto underground, Russian-collaborating agitators that had emerged. More and more I was asked where my husband was, where he had taken the boys, but I knew nothing. An incident was orchestrated in my father's shop, my mother was held up with disputes on the street, I was accosted from the far side of the street, one person spat at the sight of me, and only those closest to me would talk to me. And I could no longer count on Gergely and Anna Kátai, who had always been our closest friends, because Gergely's wife, my good friend, Anna Tószegi, who was near-term during those days of the siege, died, poor thing, giving birth.

After all this, you can imagine how I felt the moment my husband and the rest of them came home in May of '45. Oh goodness me! Sándor walks into the dusk-lit garden, opens the gate and marches in all sixteen boys in four-by-four formation. *Present arms, Levente salute*—and only when I had counted none were missing—*fall out*, all right, everyone to their own homes.

*

When my husband returned home at the end of the war, it would have been best for us to immediately move elsewhere. Although we hadn't done so until then, at least we still could.

I should have listened to my mother who had married into my father's village and always wanted to get out. She passed on her desires to me, of course, encouraging me to break out from the confinement of Kunvadas and to adopt an urban lifestyle. Mama was born a Catholic, her ancestors were members of the lower nobility and office-holding gentry of Heves County. And it was as if she thought it was merely a temporary situation, her life in this dusty one-horse town in the provincial Kunság region with my father, a wealthy farmer's son, who had put down roots in Kunvadas, his birthplace, as a well-to-do shop owner and a presbyter of the Calvinist Church. My mother longed for a city, like Eger—maybe even Budapest, but at least Szolnok—and was constantly making remarks about the dourness and coldness of the Calvinists and the slow, stolid Cuman people, who had settled there centuries ago, for whom even gardening was complex, the most they could wrap their heads around was grazing a goat. Even their celebrations are joyless, she would say, their dances are rough, their foods insipid, they've not so much as heard of wine, even the pálinka is low-grade—only their mutton stew and breaded bull trotters deserved any cachet. My mother was convinced that the all-pervading misery in this part of the country was the spawn of intellectual indolence and dull arrogance, something the local manure-scented intelligentsia had yet to comprehend.

What could be more typical, she would say, than these small-town Calvinists building a colossal church with a bell tower so enormous it can be seen all the way from Karcag, and next door, a town hall so lofty it could be a county hall—while lingering at the back wall of both is a fetid, stinking swamp. Into which backyard dung heaps are emptied, and the cesspits of traders and petty farmers, a place where the reeds conceal illegal carcass pits, among an array of discarded rusted-through basins and other scrap metal.

My mother was convinced—and this was a regular argument with my father—that to this day, the area was still susceptible to the highwaymen's bravado of the so-called Hajduks, bandits in the seventeenth century whose livelihood was looting. In whose world, one could only acquire food, drink, fodder, lodgings or a woman's embrace through endless raiding, butchering and pillaging, and when they weren't waging wars, it only led to sluggishness, crapulence and violence. The same had carried on then with the highwaymen of the nineteenth century, and even nowadays we may recognize the same outlook among the lower strata of the local folk, who, I must add, do barely scrape by in troublingly widespread, grinding poverty.

If there was any truth in this characterization—and if you were to ask me, I'd tell you there was—then the state of affairs only worsened during the war and following it, when the local council and other respectable figures had crumbled. Likewise, our own personal well-being had become insecure.

Because in hindsight, I cannot possibly ignore how vastly different my husband and our marriage were, in so many aspects, compared with the world of my parents. The fact that I had fallen in love at first sight with this tender-hearted man, Sándor Hadnagy, the salt of the earth, and his handsome, charming smile, wholly dedicated in his preparation towards becoming a schoolmaster, yet not once did he ever give me cause to doubt I was the most important thing in his whole world—my father wisely came to terms with this but it truly sickened my mother. My parents had imagined a more ambitious fiancé who might promise a greater future than could Sándor, who was actually born into a well-off local farming family, but not long after our wedding his father died, and my husband was cheated out of the inheritance by his elder brother. Previously, Mama had been dreaming of lawyers, doctors or high-ranking civil servants who hadn't squandered their family fortunes—yet her desires were cooled by my father who one day said to her, Darling, you're not the one getting married, Marika is.

As for myself, I was merely happy to rest my head on Sándor's lapel and to breathe in the scent of the lavender that he kept in his inside pocket. But it was the adorable efforts he made that left an impression, too, when he trimmed his moustache like Pál Jávor from the pictures, and flashed a suave look and a smile from under the down-turned rim of his hat, just like the film star. He knew he was instinctively better suited to this than small talk, for example, which oftener got him bogged down in some incidental topic, or got him tongue-tied at the butt of some or other wisecrack he found offensive. But this bashfulness I saw as being part and parcel of his boyish charm, maybe the only thing that did bother me sometimes was, though I would never say he was slow on the uptake, he constantly ran aground when any matter demanded a sense of humour, which wasn't my husband's strongest suit, so to speak.

My mother of course spotted this straight away and would bring it up with wry remarks, and whenever she tried to picture where I could have ended up with a decent husband by my side, Mama would, in her distinctive condescending manner, spurn my Sándor, who she was convinced didn't have the capability to lift me to a higher *niveau*. Later on, we were forever arguing about this—and thank goodness, most of the time it wasn't in my husband's presence.

So it was in the middle of such dynamics that the smears came out, when at the end of the war and afterwards they pilloried Sándor as an instructor of the Levente Movement. And then the accusations seemed to be never-ending—to give one typical example:

Through the grapevine I heard that the moment when the Communists had refused to sign our petition written in my husband's favour, what did one of them slander my Sándor with? A man put on, that even though he wasn't from Kunvadas, he was pretty sure that in our town in '44 it was the very same schoolteacher who wrote up the list of Jews to be marched off to the ghetto, and whose duty it was, more recently, to write up the list of Germans for relocation. And in the latter list, who tossed in a fair number of Jews with German surnames. Not by mistake, for this teacher and his pals very much wanted riddance of those last surviving Jews, to have them relocated abroad.

But while the others present stand dumbstruck at such a notion, one remembers that there never were any Germans in Kunvadas to begin with, so how could they have been relocated? At which the first bumpkin starts to scratch his head, saying but he read this news in some paper or other. After a spot of rummaging, he pulled it out, well, it was in an issue of the left-wing, anti-fascist *Progress*, and the headline itself stated that the story happened in Mezőberény town, so all things considered, maybe it had nothing to do with Mr Hadnagy after all.

And I could go on listing reasons, why the smartest thing for us really would have been to start afresh, somewhere where nobody knew us. We should have realized that there was no staying for us in such a troubled small town—especially not if people discovered there were indeed details of my husband's public record that easily could be attacked. But sad as it is, we didn't know we ought to be keeping our wits about us, and by the time that became clear, it was too late to get out.

*

To be honest I have no idea why my husband's hearing on 20th May came to be postponed.

People say the members of the People's Court had been given warning from more than one source (but only on Monday morning, a few hours before it was scheduled to begin), saying, some sort of commotion is inevitable, an enormous number of Kunvadas folk are marching out to Karcag with Mr Hadnagy to show support. On which basis, it's more than plausible there will be crowd pressure in the courtroom. And will be heckles and disruption too, as there was at the first instance. Because—the sources went on—lest anyone forget, that's exactly the carry-on that took place at the teacher's hearing last year. Hence, in the mid-morning, the People's Court requested that the police block the excited crowd's way with a cordon.

Block the crowd with a cordon? Did they mean to not allow the crowd into the courtroom? Or just hold it up and slow its entrance? Or to block it completely? Maybe so that it can't even set foot in Karcag town? And so would everyone be kept out or just the—so to speak—more excited section? Of course I needn't expect any answer. °

Our plan was that the appeal written in my husband's interest, signed by the two non-leftist parties, by the Democratic Women and by other respectable figures, would be submitted on Monday morning to the Karcag People's Court by a delegation. This would be led by the secretary of the Kunvadas Smallholders, Sándor's good friend, Gergely Kátai.

Later the tub thumpers among our Smallholders explained to me that the way they always understood it, the delegation itself merits an escort, besides, for them their rightful place is undoubtedly there, at the hearing, which is why Kátai organized for them to assemble directly in front of their hall in Kunvadas. What's more, they had no intentions whatsoever of inviting strangers, nor did they ever wish to get mixed up with the other parties' supporters.

But when we set off, no more than a hundred, or a hundred and twenty, to which I, too, can testify, right away at the market we were joined by a group larger than our own, and en route the crowd grew bigger yet.

Anyone we met latched on to our group and headed towards Karcag with us. Hence the conspicuousness of the soda factory's one-horse cart, being driven in the opposite direction by the youngest Rosenstein. Stopping in front of the pub, he jumped down from the seat, half-dressed but for his leather apron, and as he set about unloading and restocking the soda-bottle crates, was visibly taking stock of us too.

Meanwhile, even more folk had gathered, so by this point it was no longer just us Smallholders marching but all sorts of locals, jumbled together in a sizeable crowd. Our procession of carts and walkers must have been two hundred and fifty, three hundred strong, when it was held up by the police just outside Karcag.

As for how we could have caused such alarm, they say someone had telephoned the police station, reporting us as soon as we had gathered.

We hung idly around the town signpost—standing next to Gergely Kátai was his younger brother, Márton, and his brother-in-law, Pista Tószegi, all three exhaling garlic breath—and that's when a rather agitated bunch of Karcag residents gathered next to us, muttering that supposedly during the night two children had disappeared from their town. Others claimed the children weren't from Karcag but Kunvadas. Our people started interrogating, about exactly whose children they were, but nobody could say, just that there were two.

Cut the fucking bull!, piped up a more ill-tempered of our own denizens, OK, and what are their names?, but who could know a thing like that, just that news was going around.

And that the you-know-whos probably had something to do with it.

This remark came from a Karcag man in an open waistcoat, with a match in the corner of his mouth. Márton Kátai started nodding, but Pista Tószegi didn't grasp which people the match-chewing man was thinking of, and then Márton nudged him, Oh, come on, who do you think would be involved in something like that?

Oh, right, those people!, Pista understood, but answered, No, he doesn't think that's what happened.

Next, several of those in our company described how they did or did not believe it, people say all sorts of things, don't they? Yet as

24

they were debating, a young man with a moustache loudly assured them it was true—later they learnt that this gentleman was Zsigmond Rácz, a citizen of Hungarian Czechoslovakia who had become a resident of Kunvadas.

There's no question, this is the work of those snakes, you have my word!, Rácz kept saying, acting quite the provoker. As for Tószegi and his group, first they gave this suspicious character an earful, they think those two youngsters have just wandered off.

Might be right, Rácz shrugged. But would they not have scampered home by now?, he added. Why aren't they coming wee wee wee all the way home? Because someone won't let them. A cheeky nipper—comes home by himself.

But there were two.

Especially if there are two, says Rácz. 'Cause one would surely bottle sooner or later.

Why, know them, do you?, the group asked him, You're not even from here!

To which he replied, he was born in Bratislava, but because he's a Magyar, like them, well, he came home. After his grandparents he was left with a small plot of land on the edge of Kunvadas, so he's not a stranger around these parts. That's when the group asked his name and he answered: Zsigmond Rácz. And immediately carried on, bragging supposedly—though some say this happened during the previous day's drunken binge—that long before the war, he had joined the Slovak Hlinka Guard and taken part in anti-Semitic pogroms in Slovakia. Several say he even predicted a pogrom would break out in Kunvadas too, and that a charge would be brought against him because of it. To which he was going to stand before

25

the court and testify that he fought as a partisan against the Germans. Or that he was a member of the Soviet secret police, the NKVD.

According to our other drinking acquaintances though, Rácz introduced himself as an agent of the imperialist CIA. But he's going to tell the judge, Rácz explained to them in the pub, that he was appointed by the Russians to be the instigator of this here pogrom. With the explicit aim of undermining the area's democratic institutions by inciting anti-Semitism—I hope you can follow, says Rácz—and bring about a wave of emigration among the survivors of the concentration camps. So that as many as possible skedaddle off to Palestine, that's what I'll tell the judge.

So it's the Russkies stirring this shit up?, his audience at the corner bar tried to catch his drift.

Or the Yankees, shrugged Rácz. And the Jews.

When my husbands' supporters told me all of this, I didn't want to believe that this Zsigmond Rácz had really said such things. But supposedly he said things much worse. For instance, that when children go missing unexpectedly, he thinks it doesn't hurt to check under the nails of the you-know-whos. Because he'll tell you right now—he hates to say it—it's clear as rain who's disappearing these nippers. Or they've already done away with them because they needed Christian blood for their matzos. Sure, he remembers similar things happening in Slovakia, not just the once, and that's why a good few of them were strung up there. And pointing to the dagger hanging at his side, said that that knife had seen some use against matzo-munchers.

At this point, the older brother of one of my husband's cadets stepped up to Rácz, grabbed hold of him, propped him up against the counter and asked him: Listen up, Zsiggy, are you just talking shit or are you actually a murdering scumbag?

But in lieu of an answer, they say Rácz burst out laughing, put his arms around a few of his boorish, lumpen pals, and in chorus they started howling and wailing some obscene tune. And thus in an instant the exchange was ended, so they could cavort and screech out songs until the crack of dawn—allegedly, at one point even the famous dagger appeared, and someone effed and blinded, stabbing it into the tabletop.

*

In all truth I had no intentions of sticking my oar into this aspect of the story, but if things are flooding in from all sides in our small town, as is clear from the above, then, it seems unavoidable.

Nearly two months earlier, on one occasion at the end of March, I went along with my father up to Budapest—I figured that some experience would do me a lot of good if I did end up taking my mother's place at the shop, particularly if my husband wasn't acquitted, which would be the proper thing to do, and he couldn't teach anymore. Papa was trying to refresh the supplier contacts he had from before the front passed through, and thanks to his Calvinist clerical acquaintances, we were able to lodge behind the bombed Kálvin Square, at the same landlady's as before. For a whole week we walked up and down the town, the bombed-out streets, admittedly with little success. But it's not the catastrophic situation of supply in fashion wares I want to talk about, but the frantic hysteria, wave after wave nearly every day—and frequently crashing on us from both sides.

Looking back, this surge of high emotion was embodied by the newspaper hawkers who, even as they bombarded us with the wildest of headlines, caused anyone who heard them to lose every last modicum of self-composure. And then the other, the shower of grievances, the way I experienced it, was coming from the understandably confused Israelites who, whether they were in the street, outside our lodgings, in a shop, in a warehouse or anywhere, among the ruins, in queues, in the middle of handling official matters or doing business, fired up the debate, chipping in with their various proclamations and declarations, and so from all of their monotonous droning and irksome hammering of their arguments, for me it was as though I was constantly half-asleep, dreaming that I could hear the congregational lamenting and plaintive murmurs of an all-male chorus.

The hawkers, whom we bumped into at every step, were allegedly recruited by Source Publishing Firm, because evidently with a title like *Fresh News* it was only worthwhile putting out a paper that could be circulated as widely as possible in a matter of hours. Which, now, a couple of months after the war, was unimaginable without a host of sellers, moving on the double, shouting out headlines, distributing by hand.

A person couldn't stroll a half hour in peace among the haphazardly cleared ruins before there came pouring into the street one or other of these crier crews, announcing their arrival at the tops of their voices, then scattering every which way, to blare all over the neighbourhood: Get the new *Fresh News*! And, as is typical of hawkers, loudly broadcasting the crux of the matter right away: What do the Magyar people want? Peace, to rebuild from the ruins of the war.

Hot off the press!, thundered another with a booming voice, then roared the question: but who is fishing in troubled waters?

Yes, and who, continued a third, has been running the black market, fly-pitching, profiteering?

The war is over, shouted the criers, but who doesn't want peace? And then repeated, Yes, who doesn't, who, indeed.

Get your *Fresh News*!, called out the youngest seller, Are the returning Jews taking revenge? And then let the question hang in the air, and perhaps to let the bystanders muse over it, didn't repeat the question until he was in the next street: Are they taking revenge?

And at the same time, in the middle of the hawkers' commotion and racket, across the street some form of declaration was being read aloud by local patriarchs of said faith community. They were surrounded by a dozen men in black outfits and hats, seemingly accompanying the public announcement with prayer-like murmurings, and davening that rose and fell. I stood stunned on the corner, never could I have imagined such an Old Testament chorus, not even before, when at our Kunvadas market they used to band together as they left their temple. I seem to remember that the reading began with a date, as in any official document; according to which we, the National Presidency of Israelites in Hungary, on such and such a date hereby declare that one period of our tragedy has come to a close. The conclusion from their document was: After the great quake, for the present, we still falter where we stand, we cannot find our place.

What has been our duty in these months, members of the presidency asked themselves, because if not them, then who would answer in their stead that it was to search for and bring home surviving deportees? And to guide them back into life, someone added, then yet another: But we ought to keep the question of reparations on our daily agenda. When a third person butted in: On our agenda?—that's not enough. Sadly we would be naive, continued the complaint, to expect the state to return the abandoned Jewish goods—stolen goods, someone corrected—what does it matter if it's useless anyway, expecting them to be returned . . .

And are we surprised?

We're not surprised, they answered. But ran out of words, suddenly they didn't know what to say, and the newly arrived racket would have silenced them anyway.

Greedy, shyster traitors!, shouted a hawker in a beret rushing past us. We've always known it!, continued another with a moustache, but is it possible, that now Christian children are being corrupted at the hands of . . . ?

Of whom?, the beret looked back at him in surprise.

Well, who do you think?

Oh, come on . . . ! Are you serious?, a third nudged the moustached one.

Corrupted them how exactly?, asked a fourth.

But the beret was already shouting the next news item, Missing four-year-old! Then the moustached one cut in: Victim of a ritual killing? The synagogue's new consecration is coming any day now.

Ritual? Meaning what?, the third gawped.

Any day now—the fourth stared, as we bystanders recoiled in amazement.

We at the Israelite presidency are aware, the presidency member from before raised his voice, as once again they started citing the minutes, and preaching, as if to a crowd wider than those present, about the dire state of the Jewry outside Budapest. And this they know very well.

My foot, you know nothing. Obviously news from the faraway counties had reached the headquarters of the community on Síp Street.

Jews outside Budapest?, no such thing anymore, argued a bearded man, and then a few tried to explain, cutting into one another: There are one or two of us drifting home, but a tiny number, who barely get anything back of our personal possessions, and it's often impossible to reclaim our homes or shops in court. Well, of course, we're up against people who feel like they are now the rightful owners. Are you surprised?—well, of course they are disappointed some of us survived.

Yes, and who has been the loudest instigator working against us?, continued the speaker from the countryside, well, obviously the ones who took advantage of our deportation. Now they protest that many survivors are joining the police, but you could hardly trust anyone else.

Then it was in the 27th March 1946 special issue of *Fresh News*, published in the afternoon—I know, because I wrote down the date. While picking up the papers, the sellers were already more excitable than usual, and we understood the cause of all the jostling and chatter when we saw the headline.

Girl missing from Illatos Road!

Boy born on Falk Miksa Street!

What's that? A girl's gone missing?

On Illatos Road? God have mercy, that's where all those ghastly chemical factories are!, we started discussing the news on the street as the first people to hear. Well, God forbid, in that neighbourhood she could have fallen into a vat of sulphuric acid, poor thing.

Oh, come on, why jump to conclusions?

Well, then explain missing!

Explain missing how? She wanted to run away, got on the tram and went to Pesterzsébet! Someone will bring her back.

Bring her back?! When's the last time you saw a child brought back? In this day and age, with hardly any children to begin with?

Hear, hear! You know what's selling on the black market in France? Newborns! They bribe expecting mothers, or have someone steal the babies from us and take them abroad . . .

But the hawkers were cutting each other off and calling out that a witness had spoken out who saw the girl with their own eyes and swears to it.

That the child was kidnapped by so-and-so the junk dealer . . .

The Christian child . . .

For a ritual killing.

There you go, a junk-dealing Jew!, without an iota of surprise from the woman in the hunting hat who repeated the news as if her suspicions had been confirmed.

God have mercy, the things they're saying, muttered a young woman beside us, who looked to be a schoolteacher.

The next day of course, the *Fresh News* was out on the street again. The latest news was—according to the printed article too— that the kidnapping Jew was hunted down and taken to task by public outrage. To put it plainly, the culprit got a good licking, explained the moustached hawker to us passers-by. That the police were barely able to save the Jew from the scrum of the lynch law, that's what that means, Madame.

Fuck him to hell on Jehovah's dick . . . !, a driver wearing an armband blurted out with true outrage, shaking his head, so abruptly that none of the bystanders staring at him, including the respectable mothers, had a chance to warn the laconic voice piece of the public mood to adopt more decent language. I myself am starting to consider whether as a teacher's wife I should be recording such filthy speech in writing.

But they had already begun to present and announce the next news items. It was a quite sensational story that the Illatos Road residents had besieged the district police station. *Fresh News!* Child-trading Jew torn from protective custody! Taught such a lesson he wakes up in hospital—probably. At best.

During that night of my stay in Budapest, I tossed and turned in my sleep, so unsurprisingly I awoke at dawn with a start to the sound of the dustmen, and the bread-men on tricycles arriving with the hawkers in tow.

Fresh News, get the new fresh news! Terror on Teleki Square!

Accompanying the paper's distributor were one or two loaders from the market, a few market women, and a couple of their patrons, who were all shouting: Help! Ambulance! We've been poisoned! Suspicious brawn meat!

Suspicious how? Poisoned how?, the people asked one another.

Probably child meat.

Is she mad? What's she talking about?

What kind of meat?

Not kosher, anyway.

Come again? Child?

Ground?

By who?

Who do you think?

And the next day was exactly the same: A brand-new day, more fresh news! Calvinist pastor fakes anti-Semitic blood libel.

Libellous pastor reported!

Disgrace and dishonour!, another group's outrage rose to my window. The Jews reported our pastor!, the well-dressed middle-aged men and women chanted in raised voices. Members of the congregation of the pastor in question, we shortly found out from our landlady. Who, without hesitation, dashed downstairs to grill her Calvinist brethren as to what had brought them to Ráday Street. It turned out they weren't too sure either, each churchgoer asking the next, what accusation had been raised against their minister.

Apparently he was pinned with being the blood libel's author.

What blood libel?!

But that's outright slander, our minister is innocent!

The Reverend of our parish never spoke a word of slander.

Not even about those vengeance-breathing, bloodthirsty Jews.

Still they want to lock him up!

Eventually the hawkers tore into the street like a swarm of wasps while a stream of newer and newer headlines gushed out of them in one rising roar:

Children's flesh found in salami in Pesterzsébet house!

Child meat factory in the ghetto!

Lynching breaks out at sausage stall on Lehel Square!

Children's nails found in sausages in Újpest!

It's about time that we got out of this frantic capital, Papa and I said, looking at each other that morning, and we instantly set about packing our things so we could catch the train and get home to our own bog-aired and fuggy but still, we believed, demonstrably peaceful village.

*

In my description of the exchange that took place in front of the Smallholders' hall, I left something out. Because when Gergely Kátai and his lot were hinting that my Sándor's informers were of the same people who had returned from that almost unmentionable place, suddenly behind us there appeared a few people of that ilk. Who must have taken offence to what we were saying—that the sight of a good Magyar stings their eyes—because they retorted:

A good Hungarian, is that so?, pursing their lips. We Jews of Kunvadas know what that means, giving one another telling looks. How could we not?

And once again they came with the fabricated defamatory accusation that everyone knows Sándor Hadnagy—he was the commander of the local Levente Movement, a staunch pro-German and a reputable anti-Semite. And that he started back in '41 by reporting Uncle Berg, who owned the picture house, and who hasn't come back to this day.

Yes, I might as well say a few words on this. As in the rest of the country, in our small town of seven thousand, it has been two years since the population in question drew such a sad fate, as a result of which, from roughly two hundred and eighty, barely seventy-something made it home in the end. This followed from the laws at the time, and who could have known where those would lead?—not even they knew themselves, by their own admission.

All I know is, on 24th April 1944, they were taken to Karcag and were put out between the cemetery and the abattoir, that was the ghetto. Then on 18th June, everyone was taken to the sugar factory in the town of Szolnok, where they were loaded into wagons on the 28th. The majority were deported to death camps, a smaller number were taken to work camps near Vienna, so say the people who talk about it. And the only survivors were of the latter transport, it was from there some came home, however many were left, the less than eighty from Kunvadas.

Those who did trickle back found the displays and windows of their homes, shops, workshops and sheds broken or half-heartedly boarded up, the security bars beaten from their storehouse doors, with crude six-pointed stars daubed about the walls, some hastily whitewashed over, others still plainly visible. It was enough to just come down the main street, around the market, and left at the crossroads by the town hall to find a clutch of gutted properties, going to ruin. It's an unfortunate truth that almost everyone who returned found their house ransacked—and not just their own but their lost neighbours' too. The case was certainly that nobody in the village had counted on them ever coming back home. And only in relation to this were there any differences in people's conduct. Specifically, as to who couldn't bear watching the abandoned possessions run to waste and ruin, and who even then would never touch another person's property.

So then, regarding the protests of those who came back, about why they don't get their moveable property back, this I understand: what's theirs is theirs after all, there's no question. Moreover, we felt compassion for them and hoped they would find consolation. But it must be made clear that even prior to the deplorable events, my husband didn't think any differently.

First, I want to put it on record that not only did Sándor Hadnagy play no active role in their removal but also that he disagreed with it. In fact, he didn't support this solution even partially—for example, by joining one of the racialist parties and thus expressing passive or partial agreement. No, he was against it heart and soul, I can swear to it. Nor was he ever a member of any party, not one. He would not even allow himself to go near one, though there was a time Gergely Kátai kept inviting him.

Second, there were others who, like Sándor, deeply opposed the deportation but then in their own office—be it in the local council, in the health service, or in the police force—still upheld their administrative or other duties that pertained to the law. My husband, however, was not one of them, he had no office or any responsibility in connection with this. What's more, with regard to the matter of the mob tearing up the deportees' houses, he was wholeheartedly in agreement with Kátai and the smallholders who disapproved of such arbitrary looting from the perspective of property rights. My husband did indeed receive his orders, which as a commander of the Levente Movement he could not shirk at the risk of execution, but the sole aim of his task was national defence and did not include anything concerning the population circumscribed by the law.

Third, as concerns that particular labelling of my husband: regarding which ethnicity Sándor Hadnagy was an ardent lover of, and which he was a noted opponent of, well, any comments in this area are not merely crude generalizations and exaggerations but also are ultimately statements of slander. The way it is, my husband was a lover of Hungarians, and like most people in this country, it was in Hungary's interest that he fulfilled his humble duty, or whatever fell to his responsibility while defending our nation—which was, as it so happened, on the side of the German allies. And which meant so little in practice, for it almost only consisted of his constantly changing the cadets' location. Plainly speaking, he always led his charge of sixteen boys to wherever he was instructed by command, but while doing so he cushioned them from any danger.

And, in the end, as for whether Mr Hadnagy was indeed opposed to the you-know-whos, was anti-whatever? Had he in any form infringed upon the rights of the said people, or condemned them by virtue of their race, such an accusation might arise. Not only did he not infringe upon any rights, but in fact he defended rights—furthermore, he defended the rights of the Hungarian people. He stood up for the rights, interests and values of the Hungarian people—at times when he sensed those were being curtailed, being pushed unjustly into the background, and were thus in dire need of defence.

To mention just one example from Kunvadas. In our small town there were at least three times as many Hebrew shop owners as non-Hebrews, although they only accounted for three to four per cent of the population, if at all. And this my husband found to be unjust—not in the sense that he would have incited restriction, choking, or any such action against racially different businesses, but rather he encouraged legal, state-level support of Hungarian commerce. And that's what he expressed in the local newspaper, or stated when he had the opportunity to speak here or there.

Mind you, my father had disputes with him about this. Sándor wouldn't understand him: Well, what kind of Calvinist shop owner can you be, Papa, if you aren't looking out for your own interest in the face of the competition? But I am doing that, son, that's exactly why I'm saying it. And my father explained that in his line of business, where he represented the minority, it was in fact very advisable to respect the Jewish majority's practices, their customs, their connections, and that making an enemy of them served no purpose. Just being a Christian shop owner, in many buyers' eyes, already has its own particular advantage, it is not worth kicking up a row. One has to offer more goods, better goods, more tasteful goods than their shops—and when this works, to get ahead, but when it doesn't, to cooperate with them. Of course we have our own opinion about them—but why shout it all about the town?, this was Papa's way of thinking, and they often argued about it, because when it came to thoughts and feelings, my husband always put his cards on the table.

The widely reported cases like Uncle Berg's merely exemplify what I mentioned above. In one of my Sándor's petty pieces in *The News Teller*, he pointed to the question of why Hebrew cinema owners were so glaringly dominant in the country's network of picture houses. And so concluded that deep down they are the ones running the distribution of film copies, and so of course, anyone who was not one of the tribe wouldn't get the latest releases in time, the popular, sought-after films, in other words, would get pushed to the back of the competition. The title of the article was: 'Tell Us, Uncle Berg, Is Cinema Another Secret Jewish Sect?' Many congratulated him because they found it important and witty, but Sándor had no intention beyond creating food for thought. And in no way was he in contact with the Christian cinema owner, called Horváth, a competitor who popped up around the same time. But then, all of a sudden, Uncle Berg's cinema trade licence was revoked with reference to some sort of negligence, and so the way was conveniently cleared for Horváth. But then, the old man wouldn't leave it be, right away he spoke to his bigwig film-distributor pals and arranged that they throw a spanner in Horváth's works and he wouldn't get any films. But the old man gets reported for that, is summoned to some county authority, and it would appear he has been locked up for a while, or the whole family might have moved away, I don't know, but all trace of the Bergs has been lost. But then those of the same persuasion, they started spreading that it was of course my husband who had Berg's licence revoked, that he was the one who reported him, and had him carted off too, which is nothing but pure slander. So now this trumped-up rumour has persisted even after the war, and this constituted one of the accusations levelled at Sándor.

The other was that before drilling the Levente cadets, my husband would frequently have the non-cadets in the class (in other words, the sons of Jewish families) gather up the horse droppings from the green. Something of the sort may well have happened, so when they were crawling they wouldn't sully their clothes, but any suggestion that he would have prescribed who did what according to religion—I find it unthinkable. Besides, there were mostly cows on the pasture—which would have made for a tricky clean-up—any horses that had remained were put to work at home. So, it goes to show how seriously these accusations could be taken.

Meanwhile, in a lot of cases, we know precisely or at least we have an idea who the fiercest supporters of the persecution were. And nor can there be any question, which people, which dregs of the village had looted the houses daubed with stars. While the owners were still being filed off to the station, those people were doing rounds of the neighbourhood, kitted out with crowbars, wheelbarrows, handcarts, rags and bags, and it was not just locks they broke, but official seals too, and they took everything that moved. Not just alone, but in groups too; not just one time, but over and over again. And as I recall my own shameful memories, it's folk like these, dog-tired from looting, that constantly come to my mind's eye, clutches of drunken men, and half-full women, reciting: Oh yiddle give us your fiddle, oh yiddle give us your shoe, oy vey ah hoy oh viddle, it's the ghetto for the Jew, oy vey ah hoy oh viddle, and dry your tears dear Jews, oh yiddle give us your fiddle, oh vey ah hoy oh viddle, oh yiddle lend us your fiddle, and dry your tears dear Jews.

*

To come back to that strand of my notes that lead to the truly ominous events: we had just set off on Monday morning, the 20th of May 1946, on the Kátai brothers' carriage of course, and yet we never made it to my husband's hearing.

On the Karcag Road, half a dozen or more farmers' sons grouped around us like a mounted escort, while another couple dozen followed on carts—the bulk of the procession though was made up of those behind us on foot, about three hundred people. Fifteen or twenty joined at the mortuary chapel next to the road, a good few came from the train station too, and then at the gate to the airfield, which was in Russian hands, the last reinforcements joined, those thirty or forty-odd villagers, day labourers levelling the strip, most of whom had brought tools.

This procession of ours was held up at the Karcag town limits by the authorities. Had they not done that, my husband's hearing at the People's Court would have gone down without a hitch, Sándor would have been lawfully acquitted in due form, because he never committed any crime, we would have poured out onto to the main square, raised our hats to the Lajos Kossuth statue on the other side, and all gone home in peace. But to handle it like that, shooing us all away after such a lot of dithering, it only made for bad blood and frustration. But I must make it absolutely clear from the outset: the upheaval that was a tributary to such unthinkable assault and battery later on wasn't provoked by my husband's supporters. They were disappointed to learn that the hearing would be postponed, to learn the futility of their open-hearted protest, but never would they incite violence.

Because unfortunately, that low-life instigator Zsigmond Rácz's prediction would come true, the one he had forecast on the Monday when we were dallying outside Karcag, when we were denied entry—others say he had already begun bragging in the pub the night before—specifically that on Tuesday, 21st May, at the Kunvadas weekly market, he would set off a pogrom.

The destructive fervour couldn't be quashed until the afternoon.

By Wednesday armed forces had occupied the entire town, and people came from the Ministry of the Interior Political Department, who were allegedly being led by a colonel named Tömpe.

It's not totally clear what shape or form of resistance was organized during these hours by certain Smallholders—allegedly led by the younger of the Kátai brothers, Márton, and brother-in-law, Pista Tószegi. Maybe they locked themselves into their hall to resist the siege in case they were going to be lifted?—but the police smashed in all the windows and doors, caught some of this young bunch as they fled and dispersed the rest. The arrests and interrogations lasted the entire day.

The authorities' handling of everything was plainly brutal, at least judging by what little could be seen of the arrests about the town. We couldn't be present where the detectives were extracting statements from lifted suspects, but meanwhile witnesses were being gathered too, and neither search was able to distinguish between the two. We didn't know who confessed about whom, what they said about what, and whom the police would pick up next. The nightmare that flashed before my eyes when I saw Gross the egg seller beaten to death had come true. I was scared they would come down on us, I was scared for my husband.

Nobody knew precisely what had happened. Yet in their excitement, many were talking over one another, recounting what they had seen or just heard, but embellished the stories, made alterations, made assumptions. A lot of us had flocked over to the town hall on the day of the pogrom, in the evening, for a gathering announced as a cross-party meeting, but others only found out later and imagined a sort of public forum. What's more—since the interrogations began right after—most people got everything confused and spoke of it as though it had been one big debate where anyone could speak their mind, whereas the explicit goal was to uncover the truth and to present it for all to see. I had to resort to my imagination as well—for example, I had no notion whatsoever of what was going on in those interrogations, and so I pictured the most awful things. Surely there was plenty of yelling and beating.

And then six weeks later, at the beginning of July, the Budapest People's Court trial regarding the pogrom case began, which I sat through nearly every day and made notes, but heard a lot of things from others too.

The trial must have been into its second or third day, for example, when the judge—or rather, the official who was chairing—asked a few Kunvadas proletarians what the crowd that had escorted my husband on 20th May in Karcag had intended to achieve.

Let's see here, said the judge, flicking through the file, when we left off, you people claimed to be members of the local Communists—next, the judge identified them one by one and swore them in. And then he was interested in what they had witnessed on the street, since they had intended to join Mr Hadnagy's hearing in the Karcag courtroom.

A barefooted woman in a headscarf stepped forward and looked to the ceiling to better remember what she had been instructed to say, and recited: Well, we observed that this band of reactionaries was escorting Mr Hadnagy the schoolmaster to the hearing in a clear victory procession.

My husband? A victory procession?, I blurted out unwittingly, such was my astonishment, before being told to keep my voice down. Band of reactionaries indeed . . . !, I growled under my breath.

Yes, nodded the woman, but the police blocked the way of the crowd.

That's right, Your Honour, agreed a man beside her with his arm in a sling. Right away it was plain to see the protesting rabble . . .

Rabble is it?!, shouted somebody in the room. (Or was it in the cross-party meeting that I heard such jeers?)

The judge rapped the table and called for silence in the room, at which the injured man carried on describing what was clear to him on seeing these protestors: that the Karcag trial of Mr Hadnagy the schoolmaster must end in an acquittal, or else the jury would be lynched. Ourselves, the Communists of Kunvadas, are of the one mind on what we saw.

Who was leading the crowd?

The crowd's leader was Gergely Kátai, secretary of the Smallholders Party.

Shut your stinking beaks, you filthy liars! This contribution came from Gergely's younger brother, Márton Kátai, who later apologized to me, saying he had had to talk in that manner with the Communists because of their shameful slander. How can you pretend—he had stood up and was waving a finger at them—that in that crowd Gergely Kátai played any part, or had any say!?

Present! Gergely Kátai!—and the man in question, my husband's good friend and pal, stepped forth. I declare that the only part I played was in gathering our younger members of the Smallholders in front of our hall. I told my younger brother, my brother-in-law and my cousin, because we had been celebrating a name day the previous evening. I can't help that so many others joined en route. The crowd just grew by itself, and got louder too— because of course there were people shouting, a fair few. But I didn't utter a single word.

Yes, you did!, responded the man with his arm in a sling. You see, it was Mr Kátai the Smallholder who approached the police and started negotiating how many people could go into the courthouse with Sándor Hadnagy. And it's not just us Communists who say so, anyone who was there can testify to that.

Right, and don't forget János Cseh, the Calvinist pastor!, carried on a short bald man standing behind him.

Leader of the Party of the Hungarian Renewal?, the other in the sling looked back.

Him of course, the one who goes about calling his followers brothers and sisters, explained the bald man, paying no heed to a heckler who asked, Why can't a minister call his own congregation his brothers and sisters in the Lord?, but continuing to insist that it was the pastor and Kátai the Smallholder who had fired up the mob.

Absolute rubbish!, Gergely Kátai called out.

Anyway, continued the man with the sore hand, eventually the police said they would only allow fifty people inside . . .

And at that point I suppose I held a speech of some sort, to excite the crowd?, said Kátai, turning to face the spectators, and suddenly a smile grew across his face. Friends, how about we don't allow Sándor Hadnagy to go to the courthouse, unless we all go, every single one of us!?

Hear, hear! All or none!, we roared until the whole street echoed. Or didn't roar and it didn't echo, who would remember now.

I mean, come on, Kátai gestured to himself, would I have said a thing like that?

But truth be told, at that moment, certainly our tempers were up, and we were all worried about my husband, and like any crowd in a public space, we couldn't settle: We stand up for Sándor Hadnagy!

They'll never take the hint unless we stand strong, and put the fear into them!, somebody shouted. Because I remember this was why the police turned their weapons on us, just as we were about to enter Karcag. At which the people responded with a volley of shouting.

Have you lost your minds? Are we supposed to take on a rifle squad?!

Gutless scum!

We mean it!

Stand back!

Turn around!

They're shooting at us! Back, go back! Run!

You needn't shit yourselves! Those were just warning shots!

Friends, said Gergely Kátai, who stepped out and turned to face us, let's turn back! If this is what it's come to, and they're aiming loaded guns at us, then nor will we allow Sándor Hadnagy to go to the courthouse alone! We'll not let him go alone!

And so you see, it is clear as day to us, said the man now flailing about with his sore hand, or should I say it's obvious to us, it was Smallholders Secretary Gergely Kátai's call that this rabble not hand over Mr Hadnagy—regardless of the fact that the attorney had ordered he be brought in.

But that's a lie!, Gergely's younger brother, Márton, sprung up among the audience. And not just from where us Smallholders stand—but in objective factualness. Because the People's Court put back the hearing. And by the way, as local small farmers, we strongly request nobody confuse the youth of our farmer's society with the rabid mob! And you know what, listen up! You Communists . . .

Also known as Jews, piped up his brother-in-law, Pista Tószegi.

If you would be kind enough, from here on in, to give up trying to frame Gergely Kátai, the Smallholders' secretary, as if he was controlling every move. Not a word of it is true.

Of course it isn't true, agreed a tubby fellow from the back of the room, but remained seated on his bench. It wasn't even Gergely who spoke to the police, it was Dezső Császár, secretary of the Peasant Party.

That's right, came a voice from the corner. It was our leader, the doctor.

Yes, that was me, said the rotund Dr Császár, raising his hand. Honourable Hungarian police and great Russian army!, I said to them. Because by that time a squad of Russian soldiers had been ordered over from the airfield. I, Dr Dezső Császár, will offer my personal guarantee that if you sirs might allow our people to pass, and permit them entrance to the trial of Mr Hadnagy—which it is within their lawful rights to join—then in the courthouse there shall be no class of disorder whatsoever!

And then a fellow in a burgundy scarf jumped up and insisted that the whole story about the Smallholders being the ones who organized the Jew-baiting was complete bollocks. And the friends of the burgundy-scarfed man immediately joined in, Come on, how could anyone deny their own hard work, the Peasant Party's? Who, by the way, were once known as the mini-fascists by the . . . well, you know who.

Point is: it was mainly us decided we'd learn them some manners, insisted the Peasant Party's supporters in front of everyone.

Them and their Jewmothers!

Ah, come on . . . !

What? Why beat about the bush, eh?

So what, we were there too, so we were!, voices called from the other side. I mean, the huge mad crowd of us. Peasant Party or not, who gives a toss?

Meanwhile, I cannot understand how these people could be publicly competing over who started the upheaval and how, and over which of them was the bigger troublemaker.

Next, some heckler was shushed and order was made in the back of the room. And then Mrs Hámos, wife of Ferenc Hámos, was called upon, whom I recognized, she was again wearing that masculine chestnut-coloured suit that sat oddly on her. I remembered her as Irén Gellért from our middle-school days, then later we met in passing in Karcag, but afterwards she disappeared from our town. I didn't see her for a long time, but then the word was she had got married. In '45 she and her husband returned, as Communist Party secretary and his wife, and that was when they made scurrilous remarks about my Sándor, saying things they could not have witnessed themselves.

I want to relate, began Mrs Hámos, that when my husband and I wanted to get to the Karcag hearing by horse and cart, the crowd blocked our way and threatened us. That's why the hearing couldn't go ahead and was postponed. Well, you can imagine us standing there, and then being told to go home without testifying, without having done what we came to do. But as we tried to leave, the yobs completely surrounded our cart.

Irén, love, you shouldn't call honest working people yobs!, shouts Márton Kátai.

The bit about surrounding them though, that was true, explained Márton later, when I asked him. And just so you know, Mari, if I'm questioned about blocking their way, I'll not deny it, or deny what we were yelling: Dirty democrats, stop right there!— it put the fear into them, into their horses, I mean. And we told them straight, there wasn't going to be any kind of court trial here. You're a bunch of Jew-court arse-kissers, Ferrie. Commie Jew-agent!

Is that right, is it? Did we say that?, Márton appeared incredulous at the hearing. I don't remember saying anything like what you're saying, he shrugged.

You don't remember!? Well, your mouth was utter filth!, Irén threw over.

But who gives a fig, Mrs Hámos?, said Gergely Kátai, taking a step closer. Because if you'll pause for a second! When it comes to who shouted what in the middle of the commotion, forgive me for saying but it's completely beside the point. A crowd of people, plenty of them less than sober. Shouting back and forth—some this, others that. Me, I'd rather you spoke, Irén, of your own husband, Ferenc, who turned his rifle on unarmed individuals and opened fire on them!

Specifically, on us, on the Smallholders, nodded Márton.

What a lot of nonsense!, snapped Mrs Hámos. With that ancient lump of iron? The one that doesn't even shoot?

Any number of us can testify to your husband opening fire!, Gergely raised his voice. Yes, he did in fact shoot that lump of iron!

Did that bastard really shoot?, Gergely's younger brother gawped at him.

As the Lord is my witness, Mrs Hámos raised one hand, those were merely warning shots, into the air, because our lives were in peril! My husband would never take the life of any man!

It's a tad late for oaths now, Irén!, said Gergely. It's even in the police record: Ferenc Hámos, Communist Party secretary, points a revolver at his attackers, shoots into the crowd, and then, whipping his horses, makes his escape from the ring of people. During which

51

time, three policemen appear, who disarm him at the crowd's request.

That's right, nods Mrs Hámos, they threw themselves on him and twisted his arms behind his back, that's right. And then forced us to go with them to the Trade Association. Though I couldn't understand why. It was only once we got there I realized: they wanted to stand us up and publicly shame us, to slander us and spit at us!

And at this point the judge suddenly ended the proceedings. He thanked everyone, it was enough for him for one day, he had no more questions, could those in handcuffs be led away, and everyone else was free to leave.

But I have another question!, I wanted to shout, Please wait, will Mrs Ferenc Hámos be asked to testify? It's a matter of vital importance! Will Mrs Hámos be questioned more, or will she not be summoned again? I turned to the door, edging my way among the crowd, but by the time I got outside, I couldn't see Irén anywhere, she must have rushed off.

*

From the moment we left the outskirts of Karcag on the way back, all I wanted was to be home. Gergely and Márton Kátai put down Sándor and I at the market, so if we made a beeline across the main road we could get back to the house as soon as possible, while they would carry on round to the left—they told us as soon as they've unhitched the horses, they were going straight to the Trade Association.

Behind the church and the town hall, as it gets dark, a thick stench blows in from over the dung-water swamp, thicker than during the day. Of course I would be lying if I said this was the only reason I didn't want to go that way—the last thing I wanted was to see another person that day.

As for why the Hámos couple were hauled over to the Trade Association, Mrs Hámos wasn't the only one who was confused. As far as I know, after the cross-party meeting, during the interrogation, the investigating officer began prying into this matter. Allegedly, picking on Márton Kátai in particular about their intentions, when on Monday after the trial had failed to take place they withdrew to the culture hall.

We were there, he says, to hold a vote and write an appeal for Sándor, I mean, for Mr Hadnagy, the teacher.

The investigating officer, however, knew they already had an appeal, the one which the delegation had planned to deliver to Karcag in the morning.

That's true, replied Gergely instead of his brother, and explained, but this one we intended to send to the national leaders. Especially as it was the authorities who had blocked our right of way.

And 'cause of them Communists opening fire on us with Hámos at the head!, Márton spouted.

Who? Us? Nobody fired a single shot at you!

The point is, Gergely reiterated, we were writing up a complaint due to the unlawful force exercised by the police against us on the edge of Karcag . . .

Quiet!, the investigating officer cut them off, stating he would not tolerate any judgements made of the actions taken by the authorities. I'd rather you told me why, despite your being Smallholders, you brought the Hámoses to the Trade Association, not to the Smallholders' hall.

Because by then those gossip-concocting informers had already been taken there, answered Gergely. And we wanted to persuade them to withdraw the spew of lies they told the court about Sándor Hadnagy. But it was no use, they stuck to their statements, neither Party Secretary Hámos nor his wife would give an inch, and ignored our warnings that it could mean trouble for them.

Did you hear that?, said the short bald man, springing up. You yourselves confess to intimidation! I put it to you: Are the public here aware that in the Trade Association, in the middle of all the crowd's commotion, this husband and wife were shoved onto the stage and threatened where they stood . . . ? We honourable Communists demand our own testimonies be heard! Because we can attest to the fact that that was the moment the Smallholder rabble . . .

Who are you calling rabble?!, snapped Pista Tószegi from the Smallholders' side.

You lot! As I was saying, in the Trade Association, this vicious rabble had our party secretary and his wife fearing for their lives! Shouting: Withdraw your statements, you Communist scum!

The man in the sling took up the word then, because he could remember, this was the point the police were alerted as the legal armed forces, it was about time they stepped in. And well, he thinks the manner in which the police protected Secretary Hámos and his wife was no surprise either. Namely, they were locked up in the police barracks and only permitted to go home at five the next morning. Instead of guaranteeing their safety inside their own house. Anyway, hence they're sceptical: is that how a democratic police force should act?

And here's the clincher in this trial, the bald man threw his arms out again. Why did the police not disperse that rabid mob from the Trade Association?

Don't you be again calling a crowd of lawful protesters a rabid mob!, the Kátai brothers tried to cut the bald man off, but he wouldn't let them: Well, then what do you suggest I call the band of racist lynchers that left the Trade Association that evening for the house of Károly Würczel, secretary of the Social Democrats?

Here we go! Here comes the hymie whinging . . . !, Pista Tószegi raises a hand to his head.

What racists? We object to these claims!, said a moustached man, standing up, still wearing his cap indoors. József Konya introduced himself, adding, he admits he was the man who led the six- or seven-strong party to pay a visit to the other false witness, he says, to Social Democrat Würczel's house. That's to say, they would have paid him a visit, had he let them in. Well, what actually was your purpose? What had you promised him through the fence, through the closed window? That he wouldn't come to any harm, only to withdraw his statement.

We'll not touch a hair on his head, if he backs down, those were our words, said an unshaven fellow from behind the man in the cap.

But he didn't even want to talk to us, continued Konya. He wouldn't let us in, and he wouldn't come out himself either. To be fair, I wasn't surprised he didn't invite us in. It wasn't the first time, must be a Jewish custom. But he wouldn't even stick his beak out to see what we wanted . . . !

Well, what *do* you want . . . ?!, said Würczel allegedly. And they're still amazed I didn't want to leave my house. Should I go out? Hardly a year since what happened . . . ?! Why did I not want to . . . ! Probably because the public mood was so worked up, if that makes sense. I suppose that was the reason. And because it was night-time. And I felt like the dark was full of strange faces who were against me. Though I had never done them any harm.

But we went in ourselves anyway. We all headed in, with József leading the way, the stubbly man explained to the investigating officer. So we could put our request to Würczel on purely friendly terms, specifically for him to withdraw his statement, and as a Social Democrat to sign the petition the Smallholders and the Peasant Party had already signed.

What am I supposed to sign?, Würczel pretended not to understand us, explained those who were there.

Don't act like you've fuck-all clue what we're saying to you!, snapped one.

And don't you curse either, you hear me?, Konya kept order in his own ranks. And patiently explained to Würczel, Would you please sign this paper that officially certifies Sándor Hadnagy's political sentiments were democratic.

I'm sorry, said Würczel, shaking his head, but I can't sign this.

'Course you can, why not?

Because it wouldn't be in keeping with my conscience.

Your conscience?

Do you even have a conscience?

You, Würczel!? And so if you've nothing to cover up, why lock yourself behind a closed door?

In the end I asked myself the same thing, said Würczel after the events, allegedly. I thought: there's no reason for these people to do me any harm—so I'll go outside to speak to them. Otherwise, they'll break the door down and attack my family.

The way the others tell it, he saw that, like it or lump it, there was no point in hiding . . .

And he realized he'd fucked up with that false testimony . . .

That's when he stuck his beak out . . .

His big old beak . . .

That's it, come on out, we started encouraging him, said the others, come on out, Mister Socialist . . . !

Come on, get a move on, move those kikey flat feet!

Are you coming, Würczel?!

And then he takes a couple of tentative steps towards us, they explained, adding impersonations of how he walked.

Eventually Würczel made the decision to go along with them— he dictated this into the police record himself. Despite their manner, which offered no encouragement whatsoever. But then even his wife, whom they had frightened to death, urged him to get his clothes on and go with them, otherwise they were going to hurt him. But then when we were near the Trade Association, he says, I could tell from the way they were roaring . . . The crowd was so big

I didn't even reach the pavement! And they went ballistic . . . the second they caught sight of me . . . !

We could barely see an inch in front of our noses in the dark, and our patience was spent, Márton Kátai and his people told me— the way they remember it, they had been hanging about there for maybe three-quarters of an hour. But they were only witnesses to the whole incident, none of them laid a finger on anyone, they swear on it.

Anyway, all of a sudden we hear they're bringing Würczel.

All right, so what do we do?

What do we do?

What else? Give him a hiding . . . !

What?

Well, what did we bring him here for?

Look at him, he knows he's got it coming . . .

Best not to disappoint then . . .

Open your yap, Würczel, say something . . . !

Do you know why you're here?

You do know, don't you? And are you not ashamed of yourself?

Spreading slander about good, respectable people!

They surround me, threaten me, Würczel continued his testimony. And then attack me. They punch me, they beat me with cudgels, my head and my face. Give me bloody wounds. They shatter my jawbone and beat five teeth out of me. They batter me and kick me about so I end up on the ground, and my rib cracks. That's when I pass out.

That's right.

Like he says, said several, supporting his testimony.

Between them, I think to myself, they have admitted that the second they spotted Würczel, they lifted their cudgels, beat him to a pulp and left him for dead in the pitch-black street. Allegedly, hours passed before he came to, and staggered home so he could be tended to. But he didn't report the incident at the police station.

And it was three weeks until he had recovered from his injuries. Even then the identities of his assaulters were yet to be found.

He stated afterwards: The moment I reached into my mouth and five bloody teeth came off in my hand, I realized these people weren't beating up the Social Democrat, they were beating the Jew.

Not even beating the witness—the Kunvadas Jewry wanted to point that out, which I later read in the records. Claiming, why else would they have beaten him, other than out of racial hatred, if he hadn't even got a chance to go in and consider what he would say to the court. I have to note that I don't see the reason in the Jewry's deduction, it isn't logical.

They were still hurling insults thick and fast, continued one of the assaulted (Andor Reményi, if my memory serves me well), Würczel was lying in a ditch unconscious—nobody would help him, nobody would take him home—when the mob were already searching for some new entertainment. That's when they heard the sickening speech made by Zsigmond Rácz, the Czechoslovak national.

What form of speech are they referring to?, asked the investigating officer, after calling upon the named individual.

It wasn't so much a speech, said Zsigmond Rácz, shaking his head, as an incitement towards anti-Semitism, to tell you the truth. Now whether or not that's sickening—there's no accounting for taste. He carried on in an insolent manner, actually refusing to recall any of the events. But did admit he had warned them, Gergely Kátai and his younger brother specifically, that he was positive: During the night the Jews intend to kidnap Sándor Hadnagy, so they should post a guard to protect him.

Now listen, just between us, Gergely interjected, the chances of them kidnapping Sándor were pretty low.

No chance in hell, nodded Márton.

But we went ahead and organized the guard anyway. Eight of us took it in turns to stand watch.

Four Levente boys came out to stand watch too.

Even though Sándor himself maintained there was no need.

But at around midnight, before they stood down, added Márton in private later, Zsigmond Rácz had a word with them: Listen here, tomorrow's Tuesday, so it is the day of the weekly Kunvadas market. In the morning, all of you lot be there early because something is going to happen.

What do you mean, Zsiga?

There might just be a Jew-beating.

Whew, sure, now we're talking. We all need to be there for that. The boys said that but I don't think they meant it.

And then finally, after midnight, they all drifted home, stated the Kunvadas sergeant, who was also questioned. As for us, we still couldn't take our leave, as we saw reason for concern. Hence during the night we requested that reinforcements be placed next to our own thirteen men. And immediately at dawn the county police station sent us another seventeen men. So our numbers rose to thirty. Among them were a sub-lieutenant, a second lieutenant and a first lieutenant.

Does this make sense to anyone?, about thirty policemen were standing, armed to the teeth, on the square on Tuesday morning, so the weekly market would take place without any trouble!

*

Our fears that we would be singled out as targets finally became a reality during the night of Wednesday, 22nd May, when the police came to take Sándor away. Although they didn't put handcuffs on him—he went and stood before them, of his own accord, like the honourable man he is, to ask what they wanted of him—and although there was no rough handling as they escorted him off, still I started to tremble.

It was past eleven at night, we were just getting ready for bed— it would have been more embarrassing if we had to grope about in our night clothes and open the door half-dressed. As it was, Sándor could accept to go along with them quietly, without resistance—he didn't ask where to, and what for, they wouldn't have given him an answer anyway. He put on his jacket, and I handed him his raincoat, because the dawns were nippy still, but all he took with him were his papers and his cigarette case, and as he kissed me goodbye he whispered to me not to worry, that they're surely just bringing him in to give a statement, I would see, he would be home by breakfast at the latest. Still, I put a stick of smoked sausage between two slices of bread, wrapped it up in a napkin and slipped it into his pocket, so that if needs be he would at least have something for his breakfast. Then he tugged the rim of his hat down, looked at me from under it and flashed a wave goodbye.

As a matter of fact, by Wednesday noon we had not just suspected they would come for my husband, we had known they would. After all, both he and Gergely Kátai had been sent word they were not to leave the house, for they were to be questioned. In spite of that, Sándor and I had hurried over to Gergely's, so they could discuss what sort of statement they would hold themselves to. But from the afternoon onwards, not a soul had gone any further than their front door because the police had been in their droves, hanging around on the streets, on the roads out of town, and at the station. Two had been posted in front of our house, neither of them local.

I could barely sleep, I kept jumping awake, wondering, is that someone knocking on the window, has he actually come home or am I just dreaming? And then the time for breakfast came and went, and I could only hope he had been able to have a bite of that food. I tried to calm myself, obviously they must be taking statements from an enormous number of witnesses, and it was dragging on. Last night they were already talking about thirty or forty names they had scheduled in—and on top of that were the ones they had arrested, who knows how many.

The moment I came out onto the street, the guards immediately took a step towards me. I asked them if I'm not allowed to leave my house. It turned out I'm not the only one, nobody can go anywhere, a curfew has been imposed and is yet to be lifted. In other words, I can't go over to my parents' either, and I can't ask my father for help—during the morning the day before we had exchanged a few upset words, but we had not known then that by the afternoon our town would be under occupation. I was afraid too that those times were coming to an end, when Ignác Csóka, my formerly influential papa, could still pull strings here or there.

I thought to myself, in my current situation, Sándor will not want me to lose my head and get restless. I sat down at the table to sort my thoughts, and my mind kept going back to the cross-party meeting from Tuesday night, when the lynching had barely settled, and in the main hall on the first floor of the town hall they were already setting about uncovering everything, that is, trying to get to the bottom of things and to form their own judgement regarding those involved. Heading up this effort was our close friend, Gergely Kátai, himself being a person who had a steadfast view of what needed to be done. What they had intended was to clear up what had happened in the morning at the market, and then everything that followed throughout the town. Yet in reality, the people who flocked together in that hall were incapable of seeing anything clearly, they were like people blind and drunk from the hunt of the quarry and the smell of the blood.

I don't remember who was chairing the meeting at the point when, from various sides, they were trying to shed some light on the antecedents and circumstances of the weekly market. In the rows of the audience that same man with the arm in a sling, for example, kept his good hand raised, until—after several calls for order—he was allowed to ask whether the Communists of Kunvadas would be permitted to make their own observations for the record.

Go ahead, Gergely Kátai granted them permission, though he wasn't the chair.

And then this Communist—I know him by sight but can't remember his name—started talking about how, in their opinion, it was not just locals who had come for that particular day's market, but sellers had come from all over these parts, and from Budapest. Then his comrade, the short bald man, steps forward with a sheet of paper filled with writing and reads: By May 1946 inflation has grown so much, a kilo of bread is 150 million pengős, but people will not accept money anyway. People have started calculating in sugar or in lard, and in eggs, and are bartering goods in exchange for those. Next, the man with the bad hand carried on, taking turns with the bald man as they each said their bit, that is, though their party leaders have pointed it out, it needs repeating, the yield is low because of the drought and the peasants are struggling to fulfil their quota to the state.

In many places people are beginning to say . . .

And we quote:

Why should we deliver? Just so . . .

Their words, not ours:

That the Communists and . . .

You'll forgive us . . .

The Jews can have their fill?

They prattled on in quick succession and eventually concluded by producing some form of summative public-mood report—written locally, not centrally—which they thought faithfully mirrored the so-called latent anti-Semitism.

At these words, a murmur rippled about the audience with what sounded like a hint of indignation, which I found grotesque, considering the likes of what had been happening on the streets only a couple of hours prior.

The Communist with the hand in a sling finished his contribution with the following enigmatic sentence: Meanwhile the crowd at the market was growing and growing.

Well, I had seen it grow, after all I was standing close by. Taking advantage of the fact my husband had just got a new textbook—his fixation was that they wouldn't let him back to teaching, so he devised he would study plant health at the agricultural college by correspondence—I told him I would call in at my parents', I wouldn't be long. I just asked him to promise me that—like Gergely Kátai who was sat at home on his backside—under no circumstances would he step one foot outside the front door, because there was no question about it: trouble was brewing.

By the time I arrived, the terrified market sellers were standing in a cluster and considering whether it would have been wiser to not set up shop today. A Karcag woman who had come to sell buttons, laces and zips had closed up her suitcase and was regretting not going with her husband to Szolnok. Because there on that day President Tildy and Comrade Ernő Gerő were inaugurating the rebuilt bridge over the River Tisza, and her husband had gone along with her brother-in-law who was to take photographs at the ceremony.

Us too, we had best gather up our wares and go on home, said a couple of sellers. But then others said that last night the police had restored order, and supposedly had already got reinforcements, specifically so today's market could go ahead as usual. Order? What order had they restored, argued Mrs Sirató, if they could drag Károly Würczel from his own home and lynch him in the middle of the street?

Oh, the things you say, Jutka! What happened to Würczel?

Exactly what I'm telling you!

He was lynched?!

And he died?!

Mrs Józan the grocer had more detailed news. This bunch of yahoos wanted to get poor old Károly to sign something, but he wasn't willing, so they beat him, knocked his teeth out, and now he's laid up at home.

This is awful . . .

What bunch of yahoos? And what did they want him to sign . . . ?

Well, Kátai's Smallholders, and about the whole situation with Sándor Hadnagy, answered a man with a briefcase. And he didn't care a jot that I could hear, or who I was, though I was about to answer them myself.

Then this lot will only do the same again today!, panicked a woman who sold second-hand clothes, and sure enough, just as they were speaking the suspicious loiterers were multiplying and grouping. Lajos Sirató's wife took a look around and believed she could hear the murmur of invective. Listen to them, she said, the way they're cursing Jews, it's like someone instructed them what to say. And like someone led them here, said Mrs Józan, causing the others to start guessing who might be in charge. Eventually Mrs

Sirató spoke up again, because she thought the organizers were known. Or rather, it was crystal clear, declared the woman, that Hadnagy the schoolmaster had banded together against them, with Gergely Kátai the Smallholder, János Cseh the Calvinist minister and Dr Császár who supports the Peasant Party.

How can you say such things?, I shouted at them, because this was precisely what I had feared, and lo and behold, they were already singing the same tune.

But they just parroted on, as if by rote, that the Catholic Youth Association, the Levente Movement, the returned prisoners of war, the members of the former racial parties and the gendarmes were all being worked up against the Jewry.

Will you please tell me why you have to spread such rubbish?!, I started again, standing in front of them. And to say it to me of all people?

You? Why, who are you?

I am the wife of Hadnagy, I said, and in confusion I offered my hand to shake.

Is that right? So you must be Csóka the draper's daughter!

Mari, is it?

Yes, it is, thank you, I started again. You were saying, who was it firing up the prisoners of war and the racists against the Jews? My husband, was it?

Yes. And his Levente boys!

So, he's been inciting others against you, in cahoots with the minister and the doctor? But how could you say such a thing? I'm Hadnagy's wife, and let me ask you: Ladies, where do you think my husband is? I'll tell you: He's sitting at home. As are Gergely Kátai, Pastor Cseh and Dr Császár. They are all sat in their houses.

They might well be in their houses now—but how are we supposed to believe one word of what you're saying, Mrs Hadnagy?, countered Mrs Józan. When you've scattered seeds of hate left, right and centre?!

Seeds of hate? For Christ's sake, what is this woman babbling on about, has she read this somewhere?

Then said the man with the briefcase to her, he doesn't think the instigators absolutely need to be present, just look around the street. Clearly instigation has taken place, hatred been whipped up, but in terms of what's going down here, right now all sorts are involved regardless of party differences. Of course mostly the morally weak scum of the community.

But a clutch of people from the crowd overheard and started approaching him tauntingly, protesting:

We're passers-by—got it?! We're marketgoers, buyers . . .

Scum of the community he says!

Scum, is it?! We're local citizens! And if that's not to the liking of all you whatsits who came back . . .

The Jewish market sellers didn't need to hear another word, they have an ear for this, and come down hard at the first sign of any insinuation, saying, Don't you say one more word. And back each other up, because they won't let the anti-Semites shout them down anymore. That's right, you're scum! Anyone can see it, he says, all of you jostling about on the square here. Smallholders and

Calvinists, Peasant Partiers and Catholics, soldiers from the front, Scouts and Arrow-Crosser Nazis fresh out of internment camps, it doesn't matter which party you are.

Later, every last one of those troublemakers from the market crowd denied everything, I imagine, at least all the ones they arrested. Maybe they made claims they just witnessed the incident as ordinary passers-by coming through the morning market. We weren't there so much for shopping, they said, as for discussing the events of the night before. Because there can't have been many of us who were at Würczel's house, so you see we had to get the news out by word of mouth, of the exchange outside Würczel's, and what had happened there. And at the Trade Association afterwards, when it was dark. So that's why some of us heard one version of Károly's incident, some a whole other version.

Presumably the same people remembered different versions of how, in the Trade Association, Gergely Kátai's circle had gone about organizing the appeal they were writing in Sándor's defence. Because some said the request was directed to the Prime Minister, and everyone who was present signed it straight away, but others said it was addressed to the Minister of Justice, but they could only finish it the next morning, in somebody's house.

And of course the loiterers at the marketplace told different stories about that slimy scut Rácz's speech. Nor could they agree if he was just a slimy scut or actually spoke some truth. For example, he thought, at the new Paris peace negotiations, the Hungarian people were set to fare even worse than they had in 1920 under the Treaty of Trianon.

Listen, he says, we can demand Csallóköz back from the Czechs until we're blue in the face, but the Czechs will never give it back, do you hear?

That's all very well, Zsiga, but whose side are you on anyway? Are you for the Magyars or for the Slavs?—they said, taking the mick. But nobody could dispute that Rácz was the man putting out word to meet in the morning at the marketplace. Which is why they were all amazed when seven o'clock came and went, then half seven, and he was nowhere to be seen.

These passers-by failed to mention in their statements that a scare story from the day before had done the rounds again, I can testify to this myself, which said that allegedly some children had disappeared.

But whose children are they? Does nobody know yet?, a growing crowd asked one another. Well, of course not! They're keeping the identities secret!

You'd be good as whistling for those little ones now, poor things!

So it was, waves of unnerving and disturbing taunts, insults back and forth, regurgitations of the same terrifying scare stories, all this carried on as we lingered by the market corner nearest to the Calvinist church. And it looked like the sellers had set out their stalls in vain, because no one bought a single thing. There's no chance we're buying from a Jew now, they said.

And that was the moment Zsigmond Rácz arrived with a couple of his people. They came from behind the town hall, from out by the swamp.

Seems I'm the one you're all waiting for, he said.

Namely, Zsiga was. Who was without a doubt the brains behind this action, explained one of his pals.

Brains . . . ? croaked another.

If it's not too much of a stretch.

When shall we kick things off?

It's eight o'clock!

Right, well, I'm here now!, a grin spread across Rácz's face.

You think there's nothing we can't handle without you?, a loud-mouthed woman spat at him, whom I recognized like a bad penny. I remembered, she was called Etel Radai, and supposedly was a nurse.

Just got the feeling, Rácz shrugged, you were waiting for me. So I'll say the magic words: Let the dance begin!

From that moment, people said later, all hell broke loose at Kunvadas market. They set upon the sellers and goaded each other to grab the Jew, to wring her neck. Get the scum, for stealing our children, for chopping them up into the stew, and mincing them for sausage meat. Beat the Jew! Cut her up!

But it was too much for me to hear, let alone watch, I ran from the market square as fast as I could.

*

That Tuesday evening, I was a little late in getting to the so-called cross-party meeting in the main room on the first floor of the town hall. The Communists were requesting to offer evidence as one but weren't permitted.

Honourable members of the meeting, the man in the sling began, we in the name of the local Communist cell would like to draw your attention to the fact that, as is common elsewhere, in Kunvadas a worryingly vast number of the populace are going without provision and are starving. As a result, unfortunately, for months tensions have been high at the market concerning available foodstuffs, particularly eggs and poultry, whether they are available and for how much. Opinion has spread that market sellers have been offering these at considerably higher than their buying price. To put it plainly, the sellers are guilty of running up prices and making illicit profits. In connection to this, to our knowledge, the assault and pogrom commenced at the market when Etel Radai and her associates attacked the Grosses, the egg sellers.

No, no, not true!, jumped up Etel Radai herself, but much to our surprise not to deny it but to correct the details. They weren't the first ones we attacked! The first one we picked out wasn't local. He was some baldy called Hirsch from out of town.

Who, having heard his name, immediately stood up, because— as he put it—he wanted to volunteer evidence, he hadn't travelled home, but instead here he introduced himself, he was Vilmos Hirsch, a poulterer from Tiszaszentimre. And as he had been at the Kunvadas market since the early morning, he heard everything that the locals were discussing there. And of course, as usual, we got the odd comment that they found the chicken too dear, explained

Hirsch, but today, today they came at us with accusations that were monstrous. They were most upset about some notion that we had done away with their children. I thought I would try to make them realize the complete absurdity of the whole idea. But I got nowhere, they wouldn't listen, he shook his head. Then the moment it broke out, this whatever, this pogrom, and the whispering became a shower of abuse, a woman ran over to me—by the name of Etel Radai, I later learnt, and yes, the same woman who's present now— she set upon me and started hitting me. She said that . . .

That's right!, Etel jumped up, shrieking gleefully as she had done that morning at the market, my sister, Sándor Csurgó's wife; her boy was taken by the Jews!

But Vilmos Hirsch continued his statement, next about six of them attacked him. Within moments such chaos broke out right across the market, and it was only for that chaos, by some miracle, he was able to get away.

And then the half dozen womenfolk, who right now at the meeting were rapidly nattering among themselves, all followed Etel's lead and flung themselves at the Grosses' crates.

Meanwhile, I just stood there in the main hall and stared, feet glued to the ground in horror—as I had done that morning when I witnessed their devastation—because it didn't even occur to them to deny their actions, they were practically bragging, at the tops of their voices.

Yes, sir. Ferenc Gross and his wife. Egg sellers.

Changed their name to Russ now.

The two that came back . . .

Yes, but their children didn't.

Etel Radai took off her shoe and went at the Grosses with the heel.

No, I did not, that was a slipper.

Meanwhile we two—Gizella Bakó, and Juli, we nicknamed her The Ruskie!—we tip up Mrs Gross' egg basket.

Profiteers, we yell at them.

Tipping over them egg crates—whew, fuck me, that was . . . !

A fair number were amused.

And the squealing out of that woman, when she was trying to gather them all up . . .

Then a policeman came over, but he just laughed like a drain . . .

Constable Novák.

My own thoughts then went back to what the other twenty-nine policemen were doing during all this, the ones who had just been posted here. Later on, the Kunvadas Jewry rightly reiterated the very same question: If we may ask, where in the name of all things holy were those police?

*

As I fled the market, I ran like I hadn't run since I was a young girl. Except now I couldn't handle it, I was out of breath, and out of my wits. I've never come across such an outburst, never seen people lose their minds so, seen such a berserk, primitive horde plough into . . .

But what do we have to do with any of it? How can anyone say my Sándor was the one who encouraged them to scream such frightfully dull-witted slanders, to whip up hatred and goad each other on—even to the point where abusive language becomes physical assault? When I ran from that place, they were tipping a crate of eggs off the seller's stand. So from here on in, are we to believe that Sándor Hadnagy, a geography and biology teacher, contrived and commanded that the rabble trample the eggs, and that they spew torrents of hateful speech and destruction?

I had long known the dangers from which Sándor would need to be safeguarded. That we would have to stand united against the calumny, so any living, breathing person with some common sense and decency should testify to who Sándor Hadnagy really is, how he thinks, what he represents, how he feels. And what would be unimaginable of him. Hence we had searched wider and wider circles for signatures to go on those declarations, because I had suspected that all sorts of awful deeds would be palmed off onto one person who would be singled out and summoned before the court.

Never in my wildest dreams, however, would I have thought they would trump up some leading role for him, the rabble-rousing instigator, with absolutely no basis. I realized we had to prove that every word of this was vicious slander. But the testimony would have to come from the right person. Right now we needed someone to stand up in Sándor's defence, to give evidence in his favour, someone who had previously accused him. Someone like Communist Party Secretary Ferenc Hámos. This dawned on me as I was running, so I immediately made a turn towards their street. And ran round the back of their house, and stopped in front of the gate in the wire fence, out by the sheds, gasping for breath.

Hámos' wife, Irén Gellért, had been a year below me at middle school, but we hadn't grown up together, because they had moved here only later, and since Irén was an introverted girl, we had never become friends. Her parents were tailors, they worked together, but her father—who was rumoured to be an illegal (though we didn't truly understand what this meant), and whom I virtually never saw because he was often away, and later became a reclusive, sickly man—died at the beginning of the war. People said that because the mother ran into difficulties, a family relation took over the care of the daughter—the girl lived in Karcag for a spell. But others said Irén got married, that was why she vanished from home, in any case, after the front had passed she came back home with a child sitting on her arm. And a couple of months later her husband arrived, so they moved out of her mother's and rented out the little cottage that was now vacant.

Her husband, Ferenc Hámos, might be from Mezőtúr or Békés, I don't know, but he's not local. My Sándor knew him and had told me about him. For example, that he too had studied to become a schoolmaster but could never finish. That for a few months they served in the army together during the re-annexing of Transylvania in 1940, at first it was a triumphant experience for them, marching into our historic territories, but turned into quite a taxing railway construction. And that, back then, they already had disagreements, and afterwards, because Hámos got drafted a second time, when Sándor didn't. Later the rumour had gone around that Irén had met her husband thanks to her father's underground politicizing circles, that Hámos' family had taken the girl in, but who was to say they hadn't both been forced into hiding or hadn't cosied up to one another as illegal Communists.

I stood in the alley behind the Hámoses' house, rapping on the wooden gate, I wanted to get Mrs Hámos to come out, wanted to speak to her. I called out her name and waved when I saw someone in the yard.

Mrs Hámos! Can you hear me, Mrs Hámos? Please would you mind stepping out for a minute?

Who's that knocking?

It's Mrs Hadnagy, the schoolmaster's wife. Could I just have a word or two . . . !

Not out in the street!, said a tall young woman with a Katalin Karády hairdo, again in her chestnut-brown skirt but without the jacket, and I knew it was her.

Is that Irén? Do you remember me?

Who wouldn't remember Mária Csóka?

Yes! So you do know me!

Your face. I don't think we've spoken.

Maybe. Sorry I was so forward, I just got a shock . . .

The party secretary's wife opened the latch. Do please come in, Mrs Hadnagy, she said and withdrew behind the henhouse. Well, I think to myself, this woman's not in the mood for familiarities. But it is best, truth be told, that nobody sees us together during these unsettled hours, we agreed on that immediately, though I had no clue what she knew about the situation outside. She asked straight away: And to what do I owe the pleasure, Mrs Hadnagy?

Please, do call me Mária, won't you? I don't want to take up your time . . .

I understand. Right, so . . .

Look, Irén, you and I don't have the same viewpoint on every-thing. You two are Communists, we're Calvinists.

Well, that's a broad opening statement, if I may say so.

It's not what I came to talk about though. But about both of us being wives, Irén. Who would do anything for our husbands . . .

For our families, yes, she said. It crossed my mind she had a child, in my confusion I started asking whether it was a boy or a girl, how old it was—I learnt that he was a three-year-old boy—she felt obliged of course to return the interest. I would have preferred it if she hadn't, and in my negative response Mrs Hámos could sense how even the thought upset me. Yet it was as if she ended the enquiry not out of tact but because she already knew more about me than I about her.

So then I set out what I wanted to achieve for my husband's sake, at which, shaking her head, she tried to cut me off, but I saw she had misunderstood me, so I didn't let her: Don't worry, Irén, I'm not here to interrogate anyone about why you two aren't willing to retract your statements against my husband.

Though I have a simple answer, Mária. Because what we put down in our statements is the plain truth.

This unexpectedly smug confrontation rubbed me the wrong way, so unfortunately I straight away interrupted her: What about what Hámos' comrades are spouting at the market right now—is that the plain truth?

She replied that she doesn't know whose comrades are at the market at this moment or what they might be spouting.

Well, that my husband was the instigator of the disturbances, I tell her. That Sándor Hadnagy and his pals stoked the rabble against the Jews.

Uh-huh, and how am I to say if that's true? Mrs Hámos shrugged.

But I'm saying, it's not!

So they aren't at the market?, she looked surprised.

Irén, I'm begging!, I took her arm. One woman to another. Anyone in my position would want to protect their husband. Please, the harm done against him must be put right!

Nobody meant him any personal harm, we only spoke the . . .

Please, I'm only asking that someone say a few words for him! It's the least that could be done.

How so, Mária?

You and Mr Hámos come over to our place, no need to listen to me, everyone can see for themselves that Sándor Hadnagy hasn't put a foot outside the door! Nor did he even go to the Trade Association last night, though it was his fate being talked about. We haven't left the house, since the moment we got home from the postponed hearing.

Well, isn't that lucky!, said Mrs Hámos. It was quite the opposite for us! We couldn't even get home! Sándor Hadnagy's supporters attacked us on the way back, and pulled us away with them, humiliating us, spitting on us and threatening us! They wanted to force us to retract our statements. Didn't hear that, Mária?, she levelled the question at me. Didn't want to apologize for that, having come to my own back gate? And also for the entire night we had to spend at the police station—in the interest of our own safety, as we were told?

I just stared, and repeated, I'm sorry. We didn't know. I didn't tell my husband I was coming here, but if he knew, he would condemn such handling of the situation, I insisted. Irén! I'm begging, please, persuade Mr Hámos to see for himself, and to testify that Sándor Hadnagy is no disturber of the peace, and no instigator.

I believe he isn't, Mária, nodded Mrs Hámos, and I'll talk to Ferenc. Though I don't think he'll go out on the street today, she pouted.

Now she fell silent, lost in her memories, at which it occurred to me, to ask her if they had to keep away from this public outburst, as the Würczels did.

I don't quite follow, she looked me in the eye.

Well, I mean, are yourselves the same as . . .

Are we Jews, same as the Würczels?, she smiled. Not quite the same.

Uh-huh . . .

But why, has something happened to the Würczels?, she asked.

No, it's not that, I began to stammer, I don't know, I'm sorry, forgive me, and I could feel myself blushing. What I meant was, I said, well, especially for us, as women, in certain situations, it can be more dangerous . . .

Oh, well she truly hopes this won't be one of those situations. She doesn't want to be scared of that too . . . !

She looked at me, and I felt she knew everything about me. I stuttered something, embarrassed, she actually tried to comfort me, told me I shouldn't get myself worked up. It seemed like the whole of me was laid out in front of her, my whole past, everything I had ever seen, ever felt, all at once.

But so what is happening at the market, exactly?, she began to probe, and I answered that the situation was dire, and not just at the market. And started telling her the scenes I had witnessed right up to the point when the crowd started to yell and chased around that local seller, the bald one, and then that shrill Etel woman attacked Mrs Gross the egg seller with her slipper.

Then tell me, she said, did they do any harm to the Würczels?

At the time when she asked I didn't know much, but I couldn't bear not to tell her what little I had merely heard, half an hour earlier. Whether or not they wanted to rob them, or were looking for someone hiding in their house, God only knows, I said, I can only repeat what people are saying at the market. That yesterday, after it got dark, a whole band of yahoos went around to Würczel's house, who of course didn't want to let them in, but they threatened him, tricked him out and then they ploughed on in anyway. Then they asked him to follow them, or took him to the Trade Association, where something physical must have taken place, I'm afraid, at least that's what the grocery ladies at the market said, that sadly he got lynched, and his teeth were knocked out. That's all I know, I said, but supposedly he's at home now and being nursed.

As Irén breathed a frightened whisper, suddenly their child came to my mind again, and straight away I asked whether their little boy was at home.

No, he isn't, why do you ask?, she started, looking at me, they brought the little one to his grandmother's two days ago, when they had to go to the hearing. And she repeated her question, why was I asking?

I see, OK, I stammered, that's not why I brought it up, it's just me, my first thought is always if the children are safe. And, by the way, this isn't related either, I said—and I swear, I don't know why I had to say such a thing to her—but at the market, there was news going around that two children disappeared from the village.

What children . . . ?

Two of them. But nobody knows who, just that supposedly they disappeared.

Mrs Hámos then became so scared, she shrank. She pressed her hand to her stomach, forgive her, she has to go, she said blankly, but she kept asking me questions, about what I knew about these children. Is it two little boys?, she asked, barely able to speak, and her eyes like she was possessed by something, and can I at least tell her what age they are. I don't know, I told her, and maybe the whole thing is just a false alarm, but to no avail, she wouldn't calm down, she wanted to hear from me whether one of the children was taken by the mob that were at the Würczels' last night. Tell me, she said, did this incident happen in the Würczels' street, because they have a five- or six-year-old boy too, who was put into hiding during the Holocaust, and was only saved by the same roundabout means as little Laci.

I don't know, Irén, but don't let yourself get worked up, I said again, but it was just oil on the fire. Mrs Hámos took a step backwards, she has to go, she said, she should go inside to tell her husband, and I called after her a last time, do they believe us in the end, and will they testify that my husband . . .

But Irén just shook her head, she said to excuse her, she hasn't the time now, and she ran back towards the house.

Alone, I let myself out the back way, through the gate beside the henhouse, and without thinking, I started off back towards the market square again.

*

I still haven't got to why I didn't make it to the beginning of this gathering they were calling a cross-party meeting. I had tried to be there in good time, because before it started I had wanted to share a few words with my husband—at the same time, I'd had enough of it all, after everything I had been through that day—but as I was hurrying towards the town hall, I was held up.

I was almost at the church perimeter when a pack of women appeared before me from a side street—from the mere look of them, I saw they were coming from a lynching, and I recognized Etel Radai among them, whom I had bumped into more than once that day. I didn't want to be seen with them, and now was frightened of any interaction with them whatsoever, and of having to force my way through the clutch of filthy, stinking bodies, not only for their collective muck and sweat but for the blood caked onto them too. That was why, the second I saw them, I instantly turned in the gateway of the Trade Association, rushed to the row of privies at the back and quickly latched one of the doors behind me.

I had never been able to make either head or tail of Etel Radai— mind you, she kept popping up everywhere I happened to be— because anyone who did mention her could not be trusted either.

Never mind her endless, unsolicited prattle that you were showered with, and from which I most often made a swift escape. But it became necessary to speak to her after she had tried to save Anna Tószegi, Kátai's wife—tried to save her life, as Etel put it. Because Anna went into labour with my godchild the exact hour when the front was passing, when the Russians extended their bombing from the airstrip to the village, and allegedly Etel, not caring in the slightest about the ransacking Tartar-faced soldiers, rushed to help the mother in labour, but sadly neither the infant nor the mother survived the birth. From that day on, Etel greeted me loudly on the street—forever addressing me as the schoolmistress, no matter how much I protested—and referred to poor Anna as being our mutual friend, for whom she had risked her own life in vain, though the girl had been such a pretty mummy, who was so thrilled to be having a baby.

And now I hear the voices of Etel Radai's women in the yard— I look through the crack in the door, and there's the crew of women coming in the gate. They had the same thought as I had, for lack of something better, to spend a penny and take a breather. They clatter into the neighbouring cabins—naturally, mine doesn't open, little to their interest—and amid all the slamming doors, tinkling urine and swapping seats, a constant chatter runs back and forth between them.

Right, so what do you say, ladies?, says Etel, there's no questioning her voice. 'Cause it was us that kicked the whole thing off, wasn't it?

Sure was!, say two girls in agreement, grinning as they exit the privy.

But the women don't move on once they finish their business, some take a seat on a rickety bench against the wall, others on piles of bricks or planks, and thus carry on their excited discussion, their quick-fire conversation. They act as though they have accomplished something tremendous, have seen it through together and the whole thing a glorious success. And now, past the great feat, are discussing it, recalling details to remind each other what happened when, and exactly how it was.

Meanwhile I stay put in the privy, I sit in the thick, piercing stench, waiting for them to move on, and am forced to listen to their excited natter as they snap at each other's words. They use profanities, they are coarse and common, and I am simultaneously revolted by them and agonizingly curious. The way they talk, the things they do I find so repulsively passionate and disgusting, they are such animal females, legs spread, scratching and fanning between themselves, yet I can't take my eyes off them and memorize their every word.

Well, but the men did give us a hand with teaching the Grosses a lesson.

Sure, Bálint Zalai and the rest.

And them ones still managed to scuttle off . . .

Which ones?

True, the both of them.

The both of who?

The Grosses. They skulked the fuck away home.

No, they didn't . . .

When?

What do you not get? First we wrecked their eggs, then beat them up. And then they ran home.

I'm saying they didn't go home! Why would they go home?

For their children sure.

They've none left now!

Is it going that fast? They did yesterday!

Not like that, you idiot . . . !

Because they took in the two children of the wife's sister.

Right, when they came back from the whatchamacallits . . .

I'm saying they've no children of their own anymore.

Their own—that's true—they don't.

Supposedly they were scared them two children who disappeared were theirs. That's why they ran off home.

How would their own children disappear? Gross' wife found them in the cellar. The ikey runts must have got a fright, and went and hid.

To tremble . . .

Like a leaf . . .

I heard afterwards they had to go to someone else's to whatever. To hide.

Sure did, at our house, says a girl with a solemn nod, who has a prettier face than the rest, and smiles tenderly when she remembers the two children. Ma let them all in, parents too, four of them. Auntie Esztike came to our door saying, please, neighbour, she says, I'm begging you, hide the little ones from the lynchers . . .

From the what?

Well, from us . . .

Ma said OK at first, but then Da put her right. So in the end Ma went and told them. Because of this or that situation, you see, I have to ask you to go, get out of our house. The children, the whole kit and caboodle, the lot of you. To go back to . . . wherever, go home.

'Cause by then, word had gone round of what Gross the egg seller was after sayin'.

Why, what did he say?

That one day, all you, all you fuckin' Magyars will be done for, 'part from a few to empty our bedroom wares.

Bedroom wares?

He means you'll be taking out their crap.

Me . . . ?!

There's no mercy for that, God Almighty what a sack of shit.

They carped on for a while more, each to their own temperament, some cursing, some just muttering, others still laughing about the bedroom wares. Until Etel Radai asked the prettier girl another question:

So your ma sent them on their way, did she?

She did . . .

And they still didn't dare to go home . . .

Oh, right enough, no, heard about that.

I was there, said a girl with a higher voice.

How'd you mean?

Everyone fell silent at this question. They turned to face this barely-twenty-year-old prole, a skinny little peasant girl, head as delicate as a wren's, but as she sped through her story, her eyes lit up.

Well 'cause a couple of us girls followed them, the scramblies. 'Cause since we wrecked the Grosses' eggs we call them the Scrambled Greggs, we were in bits with laughter. Anyway, we're spying where this bunch are headed. Would have been when they left yours. The two running with their two children. And supposedly, back in the day, Ferenc Gross worked with this here chicken farmer, Meggyesi, or is that just the name of the farm, anyway, you know the one. They ran away out there, but didn't know nobody was home. And us pretending we're out on some errand. Out of nowhere but, they vanish into thin air among the farm buildings, they'd hid some place. I'll not deny, we were fuming, I mean, us their fucking royal escort, and for what. But we'd not the guts to break in after them, 'cause we weren't many, and most of us were only women. Oh, and we didn't know that the farmers, the Meggyesis, weren't home. But some stroke of luck: next door in the servants' quarters there were a load of day labourers, and others who'd come from Kunvadas, anyway, by the time we arrived, they knew the story. I mean, who to be after. That's why when we said to them there was a brood of you-know-whos hidin' out here on the Meggyesi chicken farm, the lot of them jumped up, near goin' for their pitchforks, bursting to get our hands on 'em. Anyway, we were right, the Scrambled Greggs were makin' to climb up to the hayloft of the cart house when we caught them, so they didn't get very far. Well, they'd not much luck, that ladder's an awful one for reeling about, no matter how tight you hang on, and it'll keel right over with enough help. Fuck, they flew through the air, squealin' little shits! And wait 'til you hear, do they not fall smack in the hay, and try to skitter off, like a nest of rats? Did anyone say you could go?! You'll not be giving us the slip!, we had to grab them by their scruffs and give them a right battering. No problem to us, we know how to throw our women's fists, you'd best not say a bad word, especially when there's a few Frisia branches around to help, what a laugh. The two tykes were in pools of blood after, barely movin'.

In truth, at this point, one or two women interrupted, that well, it might not be so good to bloody up such little ones, I silently watched—this girl wouldn't stand for any rebuke.

Least us women did a good job, I don't mind sayin' so myself, dealt with them more bravely than the men with the parents. Because the woman, Eszter Scrambles got a fair bit of what was comin' to her, her arm snapped, and they knocked out her egg-smeared jaw, but her husband, Ferenc, slipped out of their grasp, and shameful, let him scarper. So he could run to the farm's driveway, right as Meggyesi was comin' with his horse and egg cart. Three of the labourers wanted to block the farmer's way, sayin' we're takin' the cart to bring back the escapees. Like fuck are you takin' this cart, shouted Meggyesi, and drove into them, they'd barely time to jump out of the way. Well, can you get us out of here, István!, says Ferenc Scrambles to the farmer, who didn't understand what was goin' on first and didn't like it. But when he spied the number of us, he was scared for his cart, so let the kike heave the children and woman up to the cart bed and tore off. We ran behind hangin' off the tailboard, but Meggyesi whipped the horse up so much we were soon out of puff, and dropped to the ground, fuck all of you!—and didn't see 'em for dust.

*

I've mentioned already that on Wednesday, 22nd May, on the day of the mass arrests, my husband and I were able to make it over to Gergely Kátai's house at around noon—we wanted to discuss the message they both received that they would be questioned. And like always when Gergely wanted to seem important, he acted cheerier than necessary but eyeballed us suspiciously as he took a sheaf of paper out of his locked drawer. In the file were one or two documents from the police record of a witness' interrogation. They had been spoilt because the carbon paper wasn't straight, and thanks to a typist acquaintance we could get a glance of a few details from the interviews held the previous night, and though on the crumpled flimsy I could barely make out what was clearly the bottom-most copy of many, I attempted to read it out to the boys. I remember what immediately took us by surprise—they were questioning policemen, and as strictly as they might offenders.

The subjects, who were questioned in twos, were fairly tight-lipped to begin with, the information had to be squeezed out of them, but then became more talkative. The beginning of the record was missing, they were discussing a house the police didn't want to enter at first because they didn't know how they would be received inside.

From the next paragraph though, it was clear they were talking about the egg seller and his family, brought home from the farm by the hen farmer on his cart. One of the policemen learnt from the bystanders outside that a farmer called Meggyesi gave the Grosses a lift and dropped them home to get some rest. Anyway, so they were inside the house.

But the state they were in!—but we weren't to know then, added the second constable.

So they were scared to enter the house because the rumour was Ferenc Gross had a gun. And as village constables they hadn't been given any instruction. When they added to their statement that their inspectors had left them to their own devices, the investigating officer snarled at them, that wasn't his question, and gave them a fierce dressing-down, who do you think you are to be making accusations?

Truth be told, as I was reading the next passage aloud, it seemed so unthinkable, I almost had to chuckle in my disbelief at what these two green policemen let spill after more prompting, that it was actually the crowd gathered in front of the house who requested the constables go in and confiscate Gross the Jew's gun. But neither my husband nor Gergely found this amusing, nor the interrogating officer who flew into a rage and made them repeat the answer as though he hadn't heard them correctly. Is that right?, he says, so despite being armed police constables, you actually provided assistance in something . . . correct?!

Yes, we provided assistance in something . . .

Something to which the appropriate reaction would have been . . . ? Heh? What should you have done?

We should have . . . Right. Prevented it . . .

You should have prevented it, repeated the officer. And he prised the following from the two constables—meanwhile, reading aloud to the boys I couldn't bat an eyelid:

Sir, because the crowd was behaving in a hostile manner, because of that . . . we were more afraid not to enter the house . . .

We weren't afraid to enter . . .

Because sure why would anybody be scared of Mr Gross?

Of an egg Jew?, not at all . . . ! And where would he get a pistol from . . . ?!

We went into the house, came out and informed the crowd that Gross didn't have any arms.

Anyway . . . The state he was in . . .

Not to mention Eszter.

The police statement broke off here, on the next page it started with someone from the same crowd saying what happened at the Grosses' house. And I thought they ought to have taken statements from that pack of women I had stumbled across more than once on Tuesday, and whose accounts I heard myself in the privy in the evening.

We never did anything, we were just waiting to see what'd happen. And then we were just seeing what was going on. The Kunvadas crowd all repeat the same thing on that page.

Yes, we were waiting outside, so were were, to see if we could break in. And then out come the police, and say there's nowt to be afeard of, he has nothing . . .

All right, let's pile in . . .

Not goin' berserk, but calmly . . .

We weren't even shouting, just Gross.

Has a new name now, changed it to Russ.

Ferenc was shouting don't you hurt me, I'm a poor man like you. But for what? 'Cause we soon gave him reason to shout . . . !

Are you both constables from the village?, the report began again on a new page.

Yes.

Were you present at Ferenc Gross-Russ' house when the crowd forced their way in?

Yes. We were.

And what did you witness?

Yes, sir, we witnessed the . . . we witnessed the crowd circle around him and start beatin' Gross . . .

And somebody stab him in the groin. But that was at the end, so it was.

Some yob, a lad called Kelemen, came down on the man with an iron pipe . . .

Says: Take that, mincing Magyar children to sausage meat!

A statement had been taken from the aforesaid Balázs Kelemen, the fourth defendant, which reads:

Then in the yard I spied a 50–60-centimetre iron piping and picked it up. And when the others were done beating him, I whacked the pipe between his legs, and then I gave him two in the skull . . .

You mean to say, Ferenc Russ' skull . . . ?

Yes, two in Ferenc Russ' skull and a third in his mouth. These blows were fatal, a couple of days later they led to his what-d'you-call-it . . . they killed him.

*

When I turned onto Görbe Street on my way back from Irén Hámos', I saw poor Gross' body being carried out, beaten and pulverized beyond recognition seemingly only minutes ago.

By the time I arrived home, I decided I wouldn't let my husband know everything, lest he get carried away by some thoughtlessness and claim he's the one to intervene in the situation. Hence I only revealed to him a fraction of what I had seen, and tried to lull his suspicion. I did my best to hush him, while outside there was no cause for calm and the tension in all of us had reached breaking point.

He was to close all the windows and doors, to carry on diligently with his studies about pests and not to think of stepping a foot outside this house—but that was what I wanted, I wasn't being false. And I made him swear to this, because after fretfully turning things over in my mind for a quarter of an hour in the bedroom, I came out and announced: Maybe I'll try to go to my parents' after all. Because I can't relax thinking about my mother, by now my father must be testing her already fraught nerves, they'll be fighting like cats and dogs, locked up smack in the middle of all the upheaval. Anyway, Mama needs me, and she would be glad to know we're both safe, and it's the only way I'll settle my own nerves, so I'm going to theirs. I'll see how long I stay—until I see they'll be OK—but I ask my dear husband not to worry about me, it's only two corners, he can be sure I'll make it without any bother, and besides, maybe those high emotions have settled.

The only true part was I couldn't stay in one place. Because—I don't know how to explain it—I was overcome by an uncontrollable urge to leave, but it wasn't connected at all to my worrying about my parents. I wanted to be on the street, present, so I could be close to what was going on, so I could see what was happening with my own two eyes—and so I wouldn't be reliant on anybody else's woolly memories and fabrications. I contemplated the idea that perhaps the most useful thing would be to track down those blowzy, sweaty girls, those women flaunting their vulgarity, those repulsive heifers whom I had fled at the market when they trampled the eggs. Perhaps I could steer them back to the straight and narrow if I mingled with them.

As I came to the first corner, I wasn't surprised to see even more people than before were now running up and down the streets, yet where anyone was running and why, I had no idea. But then, I have watched ant colonies since I was a child and still can't find any order to their random movement. I did notice, however, the majority of people were flocking to the main street, near my parents' house, so I quickened my pace to press into the thick of the crowd. As I walked and looked around me, turning one way or other, not only did I notice the shape, size and hardness or softness of the incensed figures brushing past me, shoving my shoulders, my hips, this way and that, but also their perspiration, the sweat, snot, tears and spit smeared across the backs of their hands, in the thick of the haste, every wafting body odour, and every audible sound, from panting and breaking wind to a slew of curses. Elbowing my chest, clinging to my back, squashing flat my stomach, the fast-weaving bodies slowly churned out the direction the mass would break towards and move. It seemed I made it into the middle, and if I did not keep my wits about me, within minutes I myself would be pushing and shoving, shortening my steps, same as them. And then would start to make sounds similar to theirs, to rejoice in being able to breathe again, the road stretching in front of us, and us finally able to press on, where to I have no idea.

*

On 23rd May, a Thursday afternoon, as the curfew had been suspended for a couple of hours, I was able to go to my parents', but wish I hadn't. To begin with—the last thing I needed at that time was my mother's wailing verging on a nervous breakdown.

That this will never end, first one hoard lynches the other and then those ones get their own back, this lot is overrunning the village, and it won't just be the crazed rabble rounded up by the hundreds, it'll be decent folk too. And what will happen to us if your father gets picked up, and him an innocent man?

And is my husband not innocent?, I said indignantly. But me, I am to keep my mouth shut, is that not right, even though Sándor's already been taken?

My father was on the telephone the entire day, trying to reach an old companion whom he could ask urgently to find out some information through an influential acquaintance of theirs—a non-partisan member of parliament—about the reaction to the

Kunvadas events in those circles. He learnt, unfortunately, the issue made huge waves in politics nationwide, apparently on the 22nd the government held emergency debates, everyone was extremely nervous just how much of a blemish the anti-Semitic incident was on the country's image during the peace negotiations. The acquaintance whispered that the word is, upstairs they want immediate punishments, so unfortunately the case is going to be brought before a summary court.

And after hearing this, my father, instead of trying to reassure me, laid out all his newspapers, because he gets half a dozen, and from them he picked out the most terrifying criminal news stories. According to one of the papers, an armed conspiracy was uncovered in a secondary school in Baja and thirty pupils were taken into custody. In another was a story that on a train, unidentified criminals robbed a Budapest man of 80 billion pengős, murdered him and threw his body out of the window near Debrecen. And a third article reported that the summary court had condemned and executed a gang leader—the twenty-eight-year-old day labourer and his accomplices had been committing armed robbery at night.

I read to my father, though, from a fourth paper: the Baja police only found a single rifle in the cellar of one student's house, and none of the pupils from the school were taken into custody.

Just their teacher, no?, said my father wryly. And that student who was expelled so the school will have nothing to do with him anymore.

My father had me at my wit's end and I scolded him, Why do you have to torture me with these summary cases? He answered that because it occurred to him judicial prosecutions are becoming more hysterical, another sign is the increase in summary proceedings. And it worries him.

Later in the kitchen I had a fight with my mother, who had made another vile comment about my husband, and shouted at her, at which she pounced, saying only my husband could be so stupid to shout his opinions from the rooftops the very moment he ought to keep his mouth shut, and it is not just himself he has swept up in all this trouble, but me too, and the whole family. Because if I hadn't guessed, there will be a summary trial. That's right, the decision has been made but your father didn't tell you! And that tubby, bald-headed Prime Minister of ours, Mátyás Rákosi, has demanded the organizers be sentenced to death because he has to set a precedent.

I don't believe you, I snapped, that's obviously hearsay and why Papa didn't mention it. And even if there was a trial, I say, how could an accusation like that be brought against Sándor, when he wasn't even there? She should get a grip on herself, instead of making matters worse—we have enough problems already without her hysterics to boot.

But then I had to rush out because at nightfall the curfew came back into force.

*

Etel Radai, thirty-six, no children, Kunvadas citizen. Nurse. Fully trained. At Karcag Maternity Ward.

I was told this was how she described herself at the interrogation. And she added that she loves children, hence she was so shaken by what happened.

Why, Etel, what happened?, several women asked on the morning of the pogrom, the same gaggle of women I saw tramping their way to the market. The already eager women clearly imagined Etel would fall into step and tell her story. But she suddenly stopped dead and instead of a reply asked:

Happened to who?

We're asking you. So?

What happened to Piroshka? That what you're asking, girls?

Piroshka who? Piroshka Széki?

And what about what happened to me, is nobody interested in that?, Etel looked around at all of us, while I stood next to these women. She noticed me, held my gaze, and started saying how her mother beat her when she did something bad. Like when she didn't sleep. But so hard that once the wooden spoon broke.

She repeated this story at the trial, where—I remember perfectly—she introduced herself as Etel Radai: first spark of the Kunvadas pogrom. And then she started talking about the market, which she knew well since she was a child because her mother had been a seller.

But back in those days, it was just the market-women on this row, said Etel. There was no mixing. The Grosses' egg stall, for instance, was separate. Eggs always made my stomach turn. Ever since my grandma who was poor of sight beat a rotten one into scrambled eggs. The biggest shop at the market was Józan's. He sold bread too, we liked to dawdle there, because if he had any broken hunks of pretzel, he gave them to the children. And Berg and Gold didn't need stalls, because their shops were on the other side of the market. Or at least Berg's was until he was taken.

Exactly, Berg was taken in '41, cried a woman selling clothes at the market. And us Kunvadas Jews will never forget why!, she shouted to me. Because Sándor Hadnagy the schoolteacher slandered him. We never saw Uncle Berg again!

I didn't open my mouth to refute this slander, and wondered why I was holding my tongue.

Not quite, not quite, argued somebody on my behalf, because that was the Berg who had the cinema, he was the very first to be taken. The one Etel is talking about was the cinema man's nephew, who was deported lawfully in '44, with the family, and didn't come back.

But that's not true either, Etel Radai took the floor again, that they didn't come back, because plenty did. And clearly not empty-handed, because from one day to the next they got all kinds of crap, who knows where from. I could list the names. Bán, and Ferenc Gross. Sure, Weisz, he didn't come back. But the Golds came back even though they're seventy. And the two Neubergers, and the same for György Weiner and his wife and their daughter, Ilona. Then there's Bertalan Schwartz. Not to mention Károly Würczel, the Social Democrat. Oh, and what about Andor Reményi and Lajos Sirató's wife? Him from a Ukrainian labour service, her from a con-centration camp—both of them on their tod. So they throw together what they have. And hey presto, they've a child and a grocer's shop. All the while, there are others who still get bollock all, no child, no shop either, though their backs are broke for working.

You've a filthy mouth on you, I thought, but as the words were about to leave my throat, she said another name, József Rosenstein. Suddenly I pictured the man from yesterday in his leather apron, lifting the soda crates, his shoulders, his sweaty armpits, and the words stuck in my throat, I stood there, utterly mute in my own excitement. While the market-women nagged at Etel Radai: Tell us, Etel, what happened to this Piroshka?

A pensive look came across Etel, then she touched my shoulder, looked deep into my eyes and said to me in her tobacco breath: Schoolmistress, believe me when I say, I saw it with my own two eyes. The Jews gave Piroshka Széki money. So she'd bring them cigarettes from the tobacconist's. That Piroshka was born in my ward six years ago. She was only six, poor thing. I remember every single child, I'm always watching them on the street, and proud of them. But that little unfortunate, to be tricked like that. And this girl wound up in Sámuel Bán the Jew's cellar, that's where they meant to kill her.

Don't talk rubbish!, I said to her then.

But that's what happened! I managed to stop the killing at the last moment, I even reported it. The captain was stunned and asked me to show him the place where the incident took place.

What incident?, asked the women at the back, unable to hear.

Well, them killing Piroshka.

They killed her?

Several of the women elbowing around Etel were baffled. Nor did I believe what she was saying but I couldn't silence her. I moved backwards to leave them immediately.

Well, who was it killed her?

Who d'you think?

The Jews?

Which Jews?

All of them, nodded Etel. But mainly the Báns, in their cellar! Ferrie told me.

Which Ferrie?

Ferrie what popped your cherry! The locksmith, you halfwit, snapped Etel.

The Gypsy?

He's no Gypsy, he's German. Or something, anyway.

And then out of nowhere she goes on, saying she put her own life at risk, and Marika Hadnagy the schoolmistress can swear on that, and pointed to me. Because during the siege she wanted to save the life of Gergely Kátai's wife, Anna. That poor little petal, she just had to go into labour as those Russian pigs were bombing us, and so I ran to her house from the cellar of the health centre, explained Etel, but it was too late, the poor thing had already bled out. And it's them commie Russkies' fault.

And the Jews'!, someone chimed in.

Well, obviously. But I saved Piroshka Széki. That's twice she has me to thank for her life. First I delivered her. And now this.

And suddenly a woman broke the silence: Are we such asses that we'll let ourselves be taken by the sheer crookedness of this depraved pleb lying that she's a midwife?

Why would she lie though?, gaped several of the women. Where are you getting that from?

But the interrupter just carried on, It's clear as day the type we're dealing with, a notorious charlatan, a repeat offender, in fact she used to slink into the hospital in a stolen white apron and set about handing out the new-borns to their mothers for breastfeeding, but she deliberately mixed them up, causing all sorts of rows.

Then the officer puts his hand on my shoulder, continued Etel Radai, paying no mind to the ongoing discussion about her. Show me where the Jews led the girl away to, says the captain.

And so the two of you searched . . . ?

We were standing outside Sámuel Bán's cellar, Etel raised a finger for silence, when I lean to the captain's ear and says to him: Don't you let on to the Jews I was pulling your leg!

The gang of women standing on the market corner gawped: Why? Would the Jews believe it?

And so the captain says to me, All right, fuck away off. I'd be more use, he says, bringing the sausage and fatback from Gross the egg seller's pantry over to the town hall, in case they go walkies.

*

I might as well say now that this Rosenstein, who Etel Radai mentioned at the market, was an acquaintance of mine. Or, well, József Rosenstein, to whom she was referring, I had known the least, more precisely, I had known the Rosenstein brothers, in particular the eldest, Ernő, who introduced himself to me under a Hungarian name, as Ernő Rónai, and was training to be an engineer.

The family were from Kunvadas, their father once dealt in building materials, but that went downhill, so the two younger brothers couldn't continue their studies. But there was still news of the eldest, who was a student of the technical university in Budapest, though he was already planning buildings on the side, under someone else's name. As far as I remember, I had never met the eldest, so at the age of nineteen, when an engineer in training asked me up to waltz at the Karcag carnival ball, introducing himself as Ernő Rónai, I had no clue this was a Rosenstein from the village.

Nor did I know for the following six months—essentially for the entire duration of our acquaintance, I never learnt who he really was. After the first dance he merely said, quite mysteriously, that he isn't from these parts, and came to Karcag Town to visit his classmate's family. Meanwhile quizzing me, of course, do I live far, because while he's visiting, he says, he wants to meet me every day. All that came of this request was a slightly longer conversation three days later on a bench on the square, and a hurried stroll together before his departure—but over the next weeks we exchanged about four or five quite lengthy letters. I wrote them to Budapest, to his lodgings on Erkel Street, and he wrote to my address at home in the village, the string of weighty, elegantly addressed envelopes didn't go unnoticed by my mother, and she tried to get it out of me, but I didn't let spill. At Easter, we were to meet at my second cousin's so we could celebrate the traditions together, where the men would spray the women with perfume and recite a little verse, and though he couldn't make it, we were able to be together again at a dance in someone's house.

And then right up to the summer holidays, we wrote perhaps a dozen more rambling letters to each other. He wrote to me about his day-to-day life at the university, about his antics in Pest, about his hikes in Buda, his experiences at sporting events, and we debated in writing the odd film or book. But more than anything else, of course, we recalled the beautiful memories of our past meetings and discussed plans for meetings to come—confidentially, I must admit, we had all but declared ourselves to each other. The reason being that since our Easter rendezvous, we had quite literally become close—maybe I can admit that we did indeed share a kiss, and there was an unusually good, unique smell to his skin. (Of course when I agreed to marry Sándor, I burnt every one of Ernő's letters which would have disclosed all these events.) And so I happily went about my days, practically brimming with near-infatuated expectations, until sometime at the end of June the truth was unmasked.

One day, a gust of wind slammed an open window on our veranda and the glass broke. My father had his apprentice run down to the glazier's workshop, which incidentally operates from an out-building on the Rosenstein timber yard, to have them come and do the window. My father wanted to ask that the glazier, seeing as the man was here now, replace the dried-out, chipping putty on all the veranda windows, and to his surprise recognized his old colleague: the former fuel and building materials dealer, old Hermann Rosenstein, had come to do the glazing himself.

Your eyes aren't deceiving you, Csóka, it's me. As they say: When you've no more servants, see to the job yourself!

And while old Hermann was chipping away with the chisel, applying putty with the trowel, he chatted with my father—I was in the house and half-heard their conversation—and being a widower now, well of course it was most natural for him to talk about his sons. All of a sudden I catch that his eldest, he says, is called Ernő, perhaps you might remember him, Mr Csóka. He's clever enough, he's planning now to partner up in Karcag town with one of his Christian colleagues. No shame to that anymore, we're living through difficult times, are we not, Mr Csóka? My son agrees it's safer that way, and with a Hungarianized name of course: Kengyel and Rónai Planning Office, that will be their name.

Well, that's how I discovered that my own suitor was actually a Rosenstein. And thinking back, my opinion hasn't changed. Because the thing that most pained my heart and dashed my trust was that for Ernő, this nearly half a year and everything that happened between us was not enough for him to muster up the courage and confess: Mária, at first I hid the truth from you, but now I confess that I am ... and so on. And we are from the village, despite the age difference you and I might know each other from our childhoods. Please forgive me. Or something. And then after these revelations, I could decide for myself how to proceed and on what terms.

But that did not happen. He waited until I confronted him the next day, and even then he didn't apologize but fell into a muddled explanation that he had wanted to tell me about this whole complicated matter today, and no, of course he didn't mean to mislead me, the reason was something else entirely. I don't care what the reason was, I say, it's not complicated at all, the truth couldn't be any simpler. After all of this I couldn't trust him anymore, and through tears I rejected his plans. But how would I ever have believed him when he had consciously and consistently lied to my face about his background? So my mind was made up, even if the break-up didn't please his entourage in Karcag with whom we used to go to dances.

During that weekend in June, the last time I showed myself among them, we went for a picnic together, and of course straight away everyone knew everything about our falling out. And one of

Ernő's cousins was there with her brothers and her friends—among whom I happened to recognize Irén Gellért, a schoolmate of mine at middle school, though we didn't speak now either. And this cousin then asked Ernő whether I really had broken up with him. And when he confirmed it was true, she answered sarcastically:

Did I not tell you, you can't mix oil and water?

And I remember the dark stony glare of her friend, Irén Gellért, in agreement, who, without even speaking, scornfully made sure I felt just how low she thought me after that day. Ernő wrote one last letter of apology and tried to meet me, but I wouldn't be swayed. A short while later I met Sándor, and that fixed everything—Ernő later married up to Szolnok, and I never saw him again.

All else that needs be told of this story is that at the end of the war, the youngest son whom I mentioned earlier, the still-unmarried József, was the only member of the Rosenstein family to return to the village—old Hermann and his middle son Béla and his family were all lost abroad. In the early summer of '45, when I first spotted József on the street—I noticed he was walking behind me, so I stopped on the pavement to wait for him—I asked him if he remembered me and introduced myself by my married name, and then he answered none too amicably, of course, how could he not remember. I heard what happened to your family, I said to him, expressing sympathy. But I also want to ask, I say, what happened to Ernő and his family, because I haven't heard about them for a long while. That was how I learnt that Ernő and his wife, along with their two children, had all likewise perished.

*

On Friday, 24th May 1946, I wrote that Sándor had spent two nights—thirty-five hours in total—in the Szolnok police station, and I still had not got any news of him. That morning the papers were covering what happened in the village on Tuesday.

I immediately bought the county paper but got such a fright— has this reporter gone off his rocker?—that I hurried over to my father's to see what was being written in the other papers. Well, it was only more of the same. The fact that these reports had no bearing on the actual events, that's all very well, but alongside this cock-and-bull story a shower of accusations was hurled at our heads directly—and more dangerous accusations than I had feared. The titles of the articles told of a fascist anti-Semitic pogrom. Every last one of the news items referred to the News Agency's report, and though they varied in density and detail, each and every one repeated the same statements and labelling.

The so-called Press Department of the Provincial Police Head-quarters put it that the democratic Hungarian public opinion expressed deep outrage to learn of the news that on the market square, elements had been incited to attack the Jews who were present, followed by Jewish businesses and houses. According to their information, before noon on Wednesday, 22nd May, the report regarding the anti-Semitic disturbances that had occurred was received by the Political Security Department—whose name alone frightened me, it didn't sound like the kind of place with any desire to uncover the truth—who forwarded the matter to Minister of the Interior László Rajk without delay. And Rajk gave the order that a commission be appointed to probe the scene of the dis-turbances—not only to examine the events but also to arrest those responsible in one fell swoop.

As to who wrote up this whole piece and on what grounds, I have no idea, but I had to sit down, I had begun to stagger as I read on: upon arriving at the scene of the disturbances, the commission appointed by the Ministry of the Interior determined that the chief organizer of the fascist action was schoolmaster Sándor Hadnagy.

Good Lord, I knew it! What commission could have inferred such a heinous accusation and based on whose confessions? Perhaps that Communist liaison who was sent down had dictated the whole thing, who turned up in the village during the afternoon of the pogrom, and by the evening was casting aspersions at us during the cross-party meeting? And had they paid any attention to Sándor's own statement? Apparently, they had taken no notice of his words at all. Every single letter of the News Agency report had been a lie, from the first to the very last. Not only did it rehash the usual fiction in its presentation of my husband, it also introduced him with hate-mongering rhetoric:

Sándor Hadnagy had been known for his fascist conduct both before and during the war. In his position as chief instructor of the local Levente Movement, for the duration of the war, he incited violence against the Russians and resorted to every means in his assistance of a German victory. Having been reported a number of times, he was brought before the People's Court on 2nd June 1945, where he was sentenced to three years and eight months of forced labour for crimes committed against the nation. However, following his sentencing, he was released by the Public Prosecutor's Department. Sándor Hadnagy continued to abuse his freedom under the new Hungarian democracy. He kept in close contact with his former cadets and former members of the SS Hunyadi tank division.

Through his anti-Semitic and fascist conduct, he kept the democratic circles of Kunvadas in a state of constant tension.

The last sentence for example was quite plainly ludicrous—I couldn't so much as picture these so-called democratic circles that Sándor had allegedly kept in a state of tension. Of course he tried to care for his old students, but he never met anyone he could have influenced in any way. And certainly not with conduct heinously identified as anti-Semitic and fascist. Who had the gall to label him and slander him so?

It is quite typical of Hadnagy's conduct and manner of operating that on 20th May, when summoned to his own trial a second time, he used minors held under his fascist influence to organize a mass demonstration, in order to provide himself sufficient protection. The investigation concluded that during the evening hours of the 20th, Sándor Hadnagy made arrangements with his colluders to organize a fascist anti-Semitic pogrom on the weekly market day the following morning at the market square in the village of Kunvadas.

Countless witnesses could have testified that my husband didn't even attend the meeting at the Trade Association, never mind orchestrate such an abhorrent plan with his colluders. And the next day didn't step one foot outside of the house. That's all needs be said on the investigation's credibility. As for the person who framed him as the fomenter of such sickeningly base sentiments as can be read in the following sentences, not only should they be thrown in the loony bin but also sent directly to solitary confinement: In the morning hours, when the market was reasonably crowded, he began spreading the scare news that Jews were kidnapping the Christian children one by one and making sausage meat from them. The excited crowd were ordered to set upon the Jews present at the market, some of whom were severely injured.

And if that wasn't enough, to put the icing on their lie, they postulated that my husband and his people had selected in advance whom to lynch on political grounds—and naturally the author believed it was no mere chance that these people were left-wing: The methodical planning of the fascist assailants is clear to see; they weren't satisfied with the organization of a simple anti-Semitic mass action, but it was merely a pretext to take action against the two workers' parties, the Social Democratic Party and the Communist Party. One Social Democratic Party member and one Communist Party member were beaten to death. The Social Democratic Party secretary was savagely beaten. These assaults have left another three persons in critical condition and fifteen with mild injuries.

I was of the understanding three had died and the number of injured was higher. It seems those who didn't fit the story of the pre-meditated anti-left-wing massacre were left out. And towards the end, they came to the conclusion that the agitators had all emerged from the nest of the Smallholders Party or its youth section. But by stating it, the liars had revealed themselves—they had indirectly admitted that the invention of this false accusation stood in the Communists' interest. In other words, they spun the whole yarn themselves.

Upon arriving, the Political Security Department of the Provincial Police Headquarters, with the assistance of the Szolnok County Police Force, surrounded the village of Kunvadas, and after conducting interrogations, took one hundred into custody. It was revealed that the ranks of the Independent Smallholders Party and the Smallholders Youth had been infiltrated by fascist elements, supporters of Sándor Hadnagy's SS Hunyadi and Levente Movement, some of whom, as leaders of the organizations, had exploited the democratic framework in order to publicly give credibility to their fascist provocation. Proceedings against the killers and their agitators will be initiated under the Republic Defence Act. In Kunvadas, peace and order were restored due to the swift and immediate actions of the police.

So as for the court's opinion, my Monday-morning optimism had become, by Friday, fear for my husband's life.

*

Getting back to the events of the pogrom on 21st May, I left Sándor at home again, came back onto the street and allowed myself to be swept along by the excited crowd.

Believe it or not, but like at the market with the trampling of the eggs, I made no effort to avoid the band of shouting women when I encountered them, with Etel Radai at the fore again. Some might say mingling with them was plain suicidal recklessness, because I could have been listed among them by anyone had I just been spotted. Or the women themselves might have regarded me as one of them and later spoken of me as such, it was certainly possible. But I'm here now, chance led me to their company, and not only do they not mean me harm but because of Etel they also respect me, I thought, I'll not dash off. Perhaps I'll understand their motives better and maybe I can even divert them from their violent path.

Schoolmistress Hadnagy! Good morning!, shouted Etel, reaching a hand in greeting. And as though I had asked her where they were headed, she immediately started explaining, here's that Sára Józan, the grocer lady, I must know her, sure, how could I not when their shop's the biggest one, isn't that right? And she listed all the things that used to be available in Józan's shop, from kerosene and carp bream with onion to the drawstring round your knickers, and of course nowadays the shelves are emptier than a pigsty on Easter Sunday.

Etel then half-perched on a windowsill, started scratching at an itch in the crook of her knee and at her thigh, and carried on, that she thinks Sára has money stashed under her very skin. Or not, in fact, forget money, what good was a wheelbarrow full of inflated bank notes? Just gold. Who's to say of course where the gold's from? Seems they managed to stash their valuables before they were all cleared out—the village's countless needy scoured the abandoned houses, top to bottom, for nothing. So she thinks Mrs Józan must still be able to afford whatever she likes, decent products too, but nowadays they're hard to come by.

The only reason she's saying is, because after teaching the Józans a lesson, the good women best not expect any valuable loot, or they'll be sorely disappointed. As it is, there isn't much worth taking, which is a real shame, but they'll have to make do with knocking a few things over and wrecking the place a bit. Things would be different of course if they stumbled across the Józans' gold stash, laughed Etel, but forget about it, the things she's blathering, just to keep the good women's spirits up.

The words poured from her with such speed, even had I known what to say, how to divert them from more looting, I couldn't have cut her short. But just then a sweaty woman with her hair down managed to shout over Etel, but all she said was, it seems like this Sára Józan is her namesake then. 'Cause I'm Sára Tarcsai, you see, she explained. And when they were children, the same shop lady really did use to give out hunks of pretzel and stale crescent rolls.

The look on her face now though, watching us smash up all the Grosses' eggs!, laughed Etel Radai.

And her barefaced insolence suddenly throwing me into a rage, I snapped: Who do you think you are, and what have you women been up to, for hours now?!

But right away they drowned me out, and went on saying that Sára from the shop couldn't have seen everything, just the egg pelting and the cavorting about with slippers or strips of wood torn from the crates, but even so, she was frozen with shock.

So it's about time we gave her a wake-up call, Etel Radai hopped down from the windowsill. At her word they sprang up, crossed the street, walked up to the Józan's grocery shop, all fifteen of them, and rapped their fists on the door and shop windows. Their awful mouths never letting up:

This'll soon wake our Sára!

She's stood up behind the counter!

You see, here's where she's been hiding!

What Sára? That's a man!

It's her husband.

You see, you see, we found you, you filthy Jew.

We ought to box your brains out, isn't that right?

114

But old Józan couldn't hear what they were saying through the window. He pointed to either ear and held his arms out.

Oh, quit your pointing, you dangly-eared old man!, Etel shouted through the glass.

When they broke the windows, Dezső Józan no longer merely pointed, but cried out in indignation.

Seven or eight of them forced their way in and, using whatever was closest to hand from the stock, set upon the shop owner. They pelted him with carriage lamps, soda crates, lentil scoops, then poured half a sack of lentils over him, and I saw them starting to hurl the glass sweetie drawers one by one at his head. And then came the tub of lard, the axle grease, the pickled-herring jar, the sauerkraut tub, the mutton-suet pail and the kerosene keg, then they beat old Józan with the broom, a whole side of bacon, a hoe handle and their fists, and they hurled scale weights and bottles of bluing at him.

Meanwhile, I tried to yell at them but they couldn't hear me through the racket, and when they threw a hemp rope over a rafter, my voice caught in my throat and I was paralysed. But eventually the band of women had a new idea, and only wanted to cake the entire shop in a sack of fine grain whole-wheat flour.

The truth is I only saw part of all this, the majority of it I heard at the trial. Where the prosecutor listed in the same detail every item in the Józans' shop that the troublemakers used as offensive weapons.

Who, by the way, immediately denied everything and said it was impossible. In May of '46, how on earth could there be such a range in that shop, or anywhere in the village? That it sounds like a wish list—it was unimaginable with today's shortages. And even if it was possible, why would anyone have sold so many different goods in a village shop? The needy masses who had flocked to Kunvadas— how could they afford all that?

And indeed, the searches carried out at the houses of the accused indicated the same. It does appear that every member of the female detachment who called upon the shop was compelled to leave empty-handed, without any sort of plunder, quarry or spoils. Which does not mean that the rest of their testimonies ought to be believed. And I quote, they haven't the faintest idea what could have led to the entire shop being smashed to smithereens, that is, all the stocked goods and all the fittings, including the shelves, the counter, the windows and the door. The looters were less able yet to explain how the married couple could have incurred their serious injuries— the husband while in the shop, the wife in the storeroom—causing them both loss of consciousness and some permanent physical damage.

Only afterwards did I learn what these women had done with the Józans inside the shop. Personally, I merely witnessed—from across the street—their smashing and tearing apart of the shopfront, the window and door frames, too. I remember that when they finished their exhausting work, the church bells rang out. To which, as if just woken, they straightened up and went on their way.

*

On 25th May, I wrote in my diary that waiting anxiously for my husband, when there was no news, the days seemed never-ending and eventless.

And I remember it was like this for a long time.

Because I was unaffected to read about Edvard Beneš'
Czechoslovak Nationalist Socialist Party that wanted to get rid of
all national minority groups, that the party was not willing to dif-
ferentiate between good and bad Hungarians or Germans, and
hence he was calling for only Czechs and Slovaks to benefit from
full civil rights. And nor did I care that, here in our country, in
Miskolc the greatly increasing number of idlers and workshy had
been rounded up and put to work in the iron works in Diósgyőr.
But to hear that the bailiff in Kecskemét had been sentenced to ten
years, because during the Arrow Cross' rule he had not left his
position, and to read in the local paper that he had been warmon-
gering for years—truly terrified me because I couldn't help thinking
about Sándor's situation.

So instead of reading the papers, I started daydreaming,
choosing to have faith my husband would return home, a mindset
I had plenty of opportunity to practise at the end of the war. Now
of course I would have settled for less than the sixteen-strong guard
of honour and its marching in through the house gates.

On top of that, I fantasized about a court hearing where trust-
worthy witnesses gave statements which were then carefully assessed
by a law-abiding court. And that those proceedings could only result
in my Sándor's acquittal. I pictured myself sitting there and making
notes, so I wouldn't miss any detail which could be a clinching
factor towards establishing the truth—even the most seemingly
insignificant elements.

And then the time came when I really did sit day by day on the
courtroom bench. And took notes, for example, when the judge
asked the two accused standing before him:

Do you know Bertalan Schwartz?

What about him?, shrugs the first man.

Tell me how you two attacked him on Tuesday, said the judge, looking at the second man.

And the man begins his testimony:

Schwartz was minding his little shop as usual when . . .

Tending, corrects the first.

What?

Tending the shop.

Fine, does it matter? When he gets woeful news.

What woeful news?, growls the judge.

Well, about what we were getting up to, all over the village, answered the first man again.

All over the village . . . , Continue!

I'll continue, shall I? He was . . . Bertalan Schwartz was fast to act: he hurried to the railway station and secreted his personage in a freight . . .

What language is this?

What language is what?

He hid in a goods wagon . . . , corrects the other. But we weren't so slow either! We nabbed him and escorted him back to town.

Where then . . . ?

Where then eight or ten of us started beating his head with sticks.

And his hands which he was using in defence, adds the other quickly.

That's right, until he fainted, the two closed their testimony.

Take your seats.

Mrs Márton Vasvári!, the judge called on the next of the accused, and a woman hesitantly got to her feet.

But that's Borbála!, I said to myself, because I had gathered the few names from Etel Radai's mob that I knew, so I immediately recognized that this was Sára Tarcsai's cousin, or friend, or something. And her testimony is another I will never forget—at the very least for the names mentioned.

Is that you?, the judge beckoned the woman closer with a finger. Say something!

Yes.

Why did you assault these Jews with whom you never had any issue?

No issues, Your Honour, none . . . But you know, sir, when the Germans moved into town, after the ghettoization, Béla Rosenstein's furniture came to our house.

How did it get there?

With difficulty, me and my husband had to lug it home ourselves. But, we had no other furniture! And Béla Rosenstein never even came back. His younger brother came back though, you know, József, the soda-man. And since all his furniture was taken by the party, that's to say, their party, the Communist Party, so József came for mine, saying it was Béla's furniture. And took it too. That's when my husband started cursing József Rosenstein.

What's your husband's name?

Márton Vasvári.

Was he another agitator?

A what . . . ?

Don't say what, say pardon. Is your husband quick to lose his temper?

Well, he does lose his wick sometimes—but is he not right? When Ferenc Hámos is still parading about in Weisz's furs and him the village Communist Party secretary?!

Where did you learn that?

Oh, that's right, in Weisz's fur coats!, nodded Etel Radai.

I didn't ask you! On the day of the Tuesday market, was your husband on the streets, Mrs Vasvári?

That man was everywhere, I don't know where he was every hour.

Did your husband know József Rosenstein?

Yes, he did, I said so.

And did he harbour any anger towards Rosenstein?

What am I supposed to say? We were angry at him for the furniture, that much is true.

Was your husband at the airstrip on Tuesday?

Don't know, haven't seen him since Monday.

Where is your husband now?

Don't know.

He is being held in custody.

Is he?

Did you not know?

No.

Etel Radai! Do you have anything to add to this?

What I can say is, Your Honour, for weeks news was going round that the Jews were slaughtering Magyar children, and that they wanted to pave the roads with Magyar skulls. And about how good the Jews have got it all while us poor are still starving.

Did you all believe this story about sausages being made from children?

No. But we let ourselves be convinced.

And can you answer me as to why you assaulted them?

Yet instead of Etel, the answer came from another lyncher, the third friend, Sára Tarcsai. She elbowed her way to the front, saying: Want to know why? Why'd you think!? 'Cause when the Jews came back, they were poor as church mice, but now they're the ones eating white bread again. Here's me, breaking my back, shovelling muck, and forever piss-poor!

*

From one of the witness' statements I remember that Etel Radai had noticed the same church bells as I mentioned. When the looting women took their leave of the remains of Józan's shop, just torn to pieces. Is that the noon bell?, Etel looked up suddenly, and we've only got this far? When there are so many left!

But while the horde of women wavered, one of them reminded the rest that luckily they weren't alone, and that besides them all sorts of people in the village were banding together to teach the you-know-whos a lesson. And that was when the two loudest voices among the women, Sára Tarcsai and Borbála Vasvári, took turns listing names—names of people whose nails still needed checking, in their own words. When someone thought up another name, she charged to the front of the procession and shouted it in the others' faces: Gyula Vogel! Old Lajos Gold! Ica Weiner's family!—and so on. And then: József Rosenstein!—not for the first time.

As I list the names now, I am reminded of a voluntary witness who registered to speak at the court hearing without being summoned. He introduced himself as István Lazarovics, a grocer, and recounted that he arrived that morning at the village's weekly market from Budapest, but it was no protection against his unhappy fate. It took him eight days to recover from his injuries.

And then the women in question squinted over from the defendant's bench, pursing their lips. We don't remember you!, they shrugged, Get on your bike!

I bring this up because those out-of-towners still haven't made it onto the list of the lynched, because nobody knows their names, or would be hard pressed to remember their faces. But as we can see it was no guarantee the person would be spared the beating.

The hot-blooded women buzzed around their congregation like whirling dervishes, and then darted off towards Sarló Street behind the market square where Gyula Vogel, the former house painter, lived with his wife. When the bells struck twelve o'clock, some mothers among the group were reminded of their children, who needed feeding, but indeed there really was little food nowadays. So in their anger, shouting into Mr and Mrs Vogel's yard, they started searching for the supposedly missing children. Because the Vogels didn't have any children—a pair of women were debating whether they hadn't had any before, or only after coming back—it's fairly likely, nodded the women in agreement, the Vogels stole the two tots for themselves.

Are you going soft in the head? Taking Christian children for themselves? To adopt them?! Not Jews!, said some manic woman in a coloured headscarf supposedly, shaking her head. It's for something else they're taking them. For baking matzos or consecrating their temple. Anointing it with the blood, that's what for.

And then of course a couple of the women started laughing, because what on earth would Vogel need to be anointing with blood when the man's a house painter, they jibed. A soap-based undercoat, to prevent dripping, to boost the colour?—and so on.

Others at the head of the procession, calling out to the owner of the house by his first name, rapped on the windows and rattled the bolt on the gate, to hurry up and let us in. Don't tell us you're going to shut yourselves in, right in the hour of reckoning?!

Several stated that this was when, from the opposite direction, they were joined by another detachment which was larger, comprised mostly of men, their pace was faster, but who seemed to be angrier too. The women—as one later explained—would have begun by politely inquiring whether the Vogels hadn't perhaps seen the two stray boys, but these marauders came along with their supposedly accurate information and right away, without a word of warning, kicked the gate in. And they were already inside, standing in the yard when they started yelling, Give us back our children, and, This is the last time you kidnap our little ones. Soon the order was given for Vogel to bring the two stolen children out-side now, or else in a few minutes he himself would be begging to tell where they were hidden.

According to the witnesses' testimonies, the women first came across Mrs Ernesztina Ábrahám Vogel, mother's maiden name Hermina Gutmann. These names and further personal details had been read aloud, you see, between howling laughter and several blunders, from papers dug out of a drawer, by one of the girls (who isn't mentioned by name, just that she had big breasts), while Mrs Vogel herself was being dragged by three others from under the bedcovers.

However, none of them, they say, had expected what would happen next. That while hauling Mrs Vogel out of the trampled bed, Sára Tarcsai would recognize the duvet she had slept under for over a year by the scalloping on the linen. Because immediately on the day of the deportations, she had looted it from this very bed. But unfortunately, what happened was, recalled a witness, then Erna Vogel, when she did come back, headed to Tarcsai's house— someone must have hinted where to go—and asked for the duvet back from Sára. In fact, didn't simply ask, because Sára denied any knowledge, Erna stripped Sára's made bed and pulled out what was hers. You see?, says Erna, you see this scalloping?—that's my grand-mother's handiwork, I could recognize that from a million more just like it, and so on. Now, upon seeing this familiar duvet, Sára Tarcsai was suddenly reminded, anger surged through her and she started beating Erna.

You wanted your duvet back?, wailed Sára. Let me give you something in return! And pulling a rolling pin from inside the waist of her skirt, she started hitting Mrs Vogel. Well if the duvet is yours, look, eat it!, and Sára tried to stuff a crumpled corner of the duvet into the woman's mouth until she was near suffocated.

Meanwhile, the group of men, with whom they had pressed into the yard, arrived at a room that smelled of oil paints and thinner, where beneath a limey sheet they found Vogel, the husband. They twisted his arms behind his back, looped a sack cord around his wrists, and started shoving him back and forth, amid mocking remarks and roaring laughter. Now they were even asking him, Hey, Vogel, starting to remember where you hid those kidnapped children? Those two little Christian boys?

And then leading him out to the veranda, they stood him against a brick pillar, tied him to it, and even told him it was going to be his torture stake—who do you think holds up to torture better, Indians or Jews? Anyone want to make a bet?

With guffawing, yelling, the racket rose higher and higher, while they daubed paint all over Vogel's clothes and his face with round-headed brushes and whitewashing brushes, preparing to extract the answer from him with their knives. But since they learnt nothing, and must have quickly got bored of that amusement, in the end, following their usual methods, they beat Gyula Vogel to a pulp and left him there.

*

'26th May 1946. Today's news is cause for yet another day of cramps, the headline: Extensive Investigation Launched into Fascist Disturbances.' Next to my entry I attached the article, reporting that Justice

Secretary Pfeiffer ordered the Szolnok Public Prosecutor's Office to immediately carry out the most extensive investigation into the Kunvadas disturbances, and to have the culprits brought before a summary court.

And beside it was another paper's article that wrote: 'The brutal assault of the ill-fated Jewish shopkeeper was initiated by corrupted, naive adolescents. Behind them stood the inciter, a thuggish school-master, a local fascist radical, who walks free to this day, little to the honour of our public security bodies and our institution of the people's court.'

But I'm supposed to hold on to my sanity when I have to read such things! And to say that my husband is walking free. If only! We would have been long gone!

I remember in those days and weeks, not only did my misgivings multiply and gradually worsen, but one by one they all proved to be correct. Then a drop of optimism would seep back into me thanks to the occasional scrap of news. My father, for instance, managed to speak with a contact who had learnt from their parliamentarian friend that at the national assembly on 25th May, before the daily orders, a debate was held about the events in Kunvadas. And just imagine, at last they were not just regurgitating the same slanderous Communist tripe. In fact, a Smallholder and an independent representative had rejected the lies of the *Free People* and other left-wing newspapers, who wrote that the Kunvadas lynchings were organized, and done so by the local Smallholders. No evidence has been given to support this, and the schoolmaster is innocent too—protested one interpellator.

Oh, thank God!, I say.

The independent parliamentarian, searching for the causes of the pogrom, opined that the Hungarian nation barely understands a thing of what really happened to the Jewry. Given the severely distraught state of mind in which the credulous, rural population live, while tensions are heightened to breaking point by irresponsible indoctrinators pushing fantastical, anti-Semitic blood libels, then the manifestation of such beastly, murderous behaviour is a distinct possibility, and not just in one location. Hence he believes that the summary proceedings put forward in this matter should be extended to cover incitement against religious groups.

The Smallholder, however, proposed in his speech that in this case, not only were the Kunvadas police regrettably at fault for their own incapacity, but that the entire police service is also rotten to the core, for which personal responsibility can be laid on Communist Minister of the Interior László Rajk. And it's not the Smallholders Party whose role needs to be investigated but the Communist Party must be held responsible, who publicized—and here he quotes verbatim—that the people have a perfect right to be outraged, because if the government does not act, the people will take power into their own hands, and it will be the people who act. Mr Speaker, he says, the Jewish population do not deserve to endure such ordeals—when the true inciters of the Kunvadas case can be found in this very house!

Now, you can imagine the uproar this caused, said Papa, and not one of them on the left had prepared a proper rebuttal, and so apparently the whole room descended into jeering.

In the meantime, at my father's house, I laid hands on yet another newspaper, whose reporter had travelled to Karcag on

Friday, 24th May, joining representatives from the Smallholders Party national headquarters. Their first port of call was with the leaders of the local Jewry, whom they requested to take them to the town hospital, where the more severely injured victims of the lynching had been admitted. There, groaning in the hospital beds, lay people, men and women, beaten within an inch of their lives, writes the article, two are in critical condition.

We have come to ascertain just how much political responsibility can be placed on the Smallholders Party, said one of the representatives, posing the question at the bedside of a certain Jenő Burger. Who replied that the Smallholders had as much responsibility as any other party. This pogrom was caused by mass hysteria and the rabble who beat the Jews were shouting: Today the Jews, tomorrow the fat-cat capitalists!

Next, the delegation came to Kunvadas, to the home of Károly Würczel, where from his sickbed the Social Democratic Party secretary said that until now the parties had worked in total harmony in the village. The only opposition that existed was between himself and the Communist Ferenc Hámos, who was not only dismissed from his office as secretary but also expelled from the party altogether. (Which is interesting, I had no idea about this.) Then Würczel went on to recognize that the protest over Sándor Hadnagy's lawsuit became a matter of public interest, and that he reflected the village's opinion, which supported the teacher regardless of party differences. He didn't mention, mind you, why he himself wouldn't sign the declaration of solidarity with Sándor.

And indeed he gave quite a sly response to the question of how much political responsibility could be placed on the Smallholders Party: Among the Smallholders of Kunvadas, there are many people who do not think progressively, who aren't sufficiently democratic. (Oh, of course!) Which is why it might be that Sándor Hadnagy and his actions aren't suitably condemned (what's there to condemn?—what vile insinuations!), but the same is true for the members of the other parties, he said.

Was the Smallholders Party anti-Semitic?, to which Würczel answers, No.

Well then, at the lynching, which party was it that gave the numbers?

The largest part of the crowd was village rabble, he answered. There were plenty of strangers there too, who had come to the weekly market. But mostly it was members of the Communist and Peasant parties. The number of assailants might have been around thirty to fifty, but the participants were more than five hundred. But please don't ask me, added Würczel, to speak about my own party. For which many people needed only a membership card.

That's to say, even he couldn't deny that Social Democrats took part in the lynching. It was a wide range who took part in the lynching, I think he is right about that.

On Saturday, 25th May, before going to bed, however, I noted in my diary that I had called in on Papa, who had received a call from Budapest: During the afternoon, Jews had held a demonstration at the parliament because of the pogrom in Kunvadas, and several fights had broken out in the crowd. It wasn't clear who had clashed and why, all he knew was that several people were assaulted and the police had intervened.

*

When the band of women abandoned the wreckage of the Józans' shop and turned the corner onto Sarló Street, I stood at the corner for minutes, petrified, and didn't know what to do. My automatic response would have been to flee back to the house, but then I had left it precisely because I couldn't stay put with the nerves and the curiosity, and wanted to be a witness.

And suddenly I remembered Irén Gellért, now Mrs Hámos, whom I had called on barely an hour ago. Irén had hurried off to her mother's out of worry for her child. But did she make it? Shouldn't I check how they were?

I tried to jog my memory as to where her mother, the widowed Mrs Gellért lived, somewhere nearby, not far. When I was a little girl, we avoided their street because we were told that that house was an 'illegal' house, just as we were told about 'Jewish' houses, which we also never dreamt of entering, though we didn't really know what either expression meant.

And suddenly there I was, in front of the illegal place, Mrs Gellért's house. I must warn her, I thought. I must ask her whether her grandson is still here, and whether Irén, her daughter too. And whether they've found a good hiding place, because the people who could break in any moment now, they aren't mucking about. But if I start making a racket, knocking at the windows and doors, I'll only scare Mrs Gellért and I can be sure she won't open the door—such was my train of thought.

I never would have believed—being a far cry beyond my youth and wearing a skirt—that I would be capable of grabbing the top edge of the high fence, hoisting myself up, standing on the handle of the gate, putting one leg over the wooden boards, then the other, and jumping from the top into the flowerbed. Into a strange house, an illegal house. That I would bring myself to do it after only a moment's hesitation, finally decided by my own fear, as I spotted the advance party of the familiar horde of women coming around the corner. It was here, standing in the garden, I truly became terrified, partly at the coming women, partly at the difficulty of explaining the situation.

But I couldn't wait here to see whether Mrs Gellért would answer or not. They could have broken the gate down at any moment—I swore I could hear their voices—so I stole into the kitchen. And straight away found her there, the old woman was standing behind the door, pale as a ghost, she had been watching me from behind the curtain.

I quickly apologized for climbing into the garden, I just wanted to warn you, I say, and asked, Are you alone, is your daughter here and your grandson? She shook her head, bewildered, and I suggested that we hide, as well as we possibly can.

To which she shuffled about in distress like she needed to go to the loo, she couldn't decide where to suggest as a hiding place, and eventually opened the wardrobe door for me.

Well, that won't do, I shook my head, that's the first place they'll check. But you know what?, and I stood up straight. We'll not hide at all. We'll sit at the table, I say, and we'll just peel these potatoes— and then I picked up the proofing basket from behind the stool. Can I have a knife please!

Both of us were peeling our second potato when the intruders slammed in the gate. The old woman gave a start, she made to run but I grabbed her arm, don't be scared, I'll talk to them.

I stood up, leant against the kitchen doorpost, and when they came towards me, I spoke.

Hang on one second, ladies!, I told them, Do you not recognize me? We were only just speaking this morning on the market square. Etel Radai called me the schoolmistress, do you not remember? I don't see Etel with you, but surely you don't mean to come ploughing through me? Do you not see you've got the wrong place? It's my own friend that lives here with her mother. I don't think you'd be wanting to harm either of them.

At which they shoved me in the chest and I stumbled back to the middle of the kitchen, barely keeping my balance. In my terror I started shouting, repeating my name, but they weren't interested. Nor did they want to remember they had ever seen me, though I certainly remembered them, but unfortunately knew none of them by name.

And then I was slapped twice, out of nowhere, followed by a painful kick to the shinbone, I doubled over, and someone—with both fists I assume, extremely hard—struck me on the back of the neck. As I fell I heard a man grunting, Jew-whore, but then everything went dark.

Slowly coming round, but still uncertain what was dream and what was reality, I became conscious of a hefty, reeking body clutching at my belly, trying to force a knee between my thighs and rummaging under my skirt. Though I seemed to be quite far from regaining my senses, I could remember: this has happened before, it's happening again.

Back then, that fetid, Tatar-faced animal in a shell jacket wasn't even flustered, he was so strong, razor-sharp and so fast, there was nothing I could do—I won't go into the details. This was already more than I could bear to admit to my husband afterwards. Eventually, Sándor stopped interrogating me and all he said was, in that situation I have to break one of their fingers, that will soon rid them of any desire. And as I was just on the verge of waking, rising back to consciousness, suddenly the advice sprung to my mind.

Just then the old woman appeared above my head, shrieking furiously, holding a whetstone, and beat the head of the ape lying on top of me, while I grabbed the index finger prodding into my breast, gripped tight with both hands so he couldn't pull it away, and summoning all my strength, yanked it back until I felt the crack in the palm of my hand. He was already screaming, thank God, it worked.

I dragged myself from under him, while I was still coming to life, and when the sharp pain shot through my head, realized they must have knocked me to the floor. Seemingly now that we really were in danger, the old woman had a better idea, she pulled me into the pantry, and as I locked the door from the inside, a surprisingly pleasant smell caught my nose. Glancing around, I saw the lock appeared to be a powerful, ancient lump, the door humungous too, and hanging on the wall, a row of drying lavender bunches. Of course, this was what I had smelt when she showed me the wardrobe. I pulled down a handful of lavender for myself and stuffed it in my skirt pocket.

To our surprise though, nobody battered the door. That wild beast outside howled a while, but luckily he was alone, his companions didn't rush to his aid, so he soon cleared off.

Only now did the old woman dare to speak again, through tears guessing what might have happened to her husband.

Oh, do you have a husband?

I do, yes, they must have found him quick, he ran out of the house, but I'm sure they caught him. Because he's seventy-three years old, my Lajos.

Which Lajos is that?

Lajos Gold, the ironmonger.

But the old woman didn't let me a moment to query whether she was or wasn't Mrs Gellért, because outside it was as quiet as the grave, she unlocked the door and rushed out of the house. She looked around the yard but didn't see her husband, only the shards of plates and soup bowls, flung out the door, and the overturned chicken coop. She went out to the street, and Mr Gold was lying half prone, his legs twisted, in a ditch in front of the house. Blood was trickling from his ear. The old woman kneeled beside him, tears streaming down her face, and cupped his face in her hands.

At which Gold opened his eyes. I recognized your touch, he said, and smiled.

Are you OK?

And you?

Does it hurt a lot?

I played dead, said Gold. And after a while they lost interest. They left me.

At the hearing, apparently the following statements were taken on record:

We pulled the seventy-three-year-old Lajos Gold out onto the street and assaulted him there. He escaped any further—possibly fatal—blows because we took him for dead. We beat his wife exactly the same. And the son too, returning home at the news of his parents' attack.

I had not heard about a son. Their son didn't appear at the Golds' house while I was there, he must have been caught on the corner.

Had I to explain why I never told a soul, not even my husband, about that half hour I spent in the Golds' house, I don't think I could. By all means I have written it down here, but who's to say I will ever show this to anyone.

*

According to my diary, my husband's trial began on 4th June 1946 in Szolnok. I can barely bring myself to write, so goes the entry, Sándor has been innocently brought before a summary court as an alleged instigator, alongside his friend Gergely Kátai. And six more of the lynching's culprits. When such a reprisal was first rumoured, many of us initially took it to be a scare story, but the threat of a summary jurisdiction against Sándor and Gergely became more plausible by the day until it really happened.

The summary court had to make their decision within seventy-two hours, of which nearly forty had passed when I jotted down that for two days I had been sitting in the park on a bench, because they wouldn't let me into the trial. I privately ranted about how we could have come to this, what a mockery it was of law and justice, but there was no sense in insisting, it was plainly judicial murder. I spent the night shivering in the train station scared to death, attempting to find relief in making notes. And then I took out Sándor's white handkerchief—I had folded up the lavender bunch from the Golds', so that when my spirits needed lifting, I could breathe in its fragrant smell.

Counting the hours, it occurred to me one person had actually offered some compassion a couple of days after the news of the summary court hearing became public: Irén, the wife of Ferenc Hámos, the Communist Party secretary, visited me that evening to tell me they were moving to the city of Miskolc, and she didn't want to leave me in the present situation without saying goodbye.

I was pleased she came, it was a genuine surprise. Especially because on the day of the pogrom, in the evening of the cross-party meeting, I ran into Irén, who watched the whole song and dance from the gallery and was naturally thoroughly upset by what she heard.

I didn't think after those statements she would ever be sympathetic towards me again, and now here she was—I suppose the threat of a summary court hearing was reason enough. She just came to say goodbye, and to tell me how sorry she was to hear what was being done to my husband. Touched, I accompanied her to the gate to see her off and wish her well.

My head was so muddled, it wasn't until the next day I remembered dearest Irén could have offered more than kind sympathy after all. Because had I not already requested her help when I called at her door—how could I have forgotten?! I asked her to testify with Hámos at my husband's trial.

At around noon I hurried to their house but they were already on their way. Luckily Irén had left their new address in Miskolc on a note and I quickly wrote to them, that the summary trial begins a week later in Szolnok, I would be grateful if they both came forward as witnesses.

Sitting on the bench in Szolnok, I remembered how I had waited in vain for their help, everything turned out to be empty promises.

But I could eventually breathe a sigh of relief when, thank God, some five hours later, the judgement was suspended. The summary court proclaimed that since during the seventy-two hours they had not successfully pinpointed the instigators, the case would be referred to the proper procedure. Some sort of public prosecutor straight away arranged for the case to be heard by the Budapest People's Court. In other words, not a proper procedure at all, but another people's court. At least it wasn't a summary proceeding. It was fixed to begin 3rd July.

As we had not been allowed to enter the courtroom, I hadn't seen Sándor at all, not even in the corridor. They were covertly smuggled between the courtroom and their holding cells, when the very reason I stayed in Szolnok until the end was in case we could meet, fleetingly even, and I could give him a few packs of cigarettes, or at the very least we could glimpse each other.

*

I didn't write it into my diary at the time, but in Szolnok, on the morning the trial was adjourned, on my way towards the court-house, in the street I saw a police officer leading three fettered figures in worn suits—boards hanging around their necks pronounced that these unfortunates were hoarding, profiteering and racketeering spongers. The rabble followed in tow, twenty to thirty strong—they didn't mince their words, taking their cues from the boards of shame, but not missing an opportunity for a few anti-Jewish slurs.

As I looked on, a well-informed market woman began filling me in, but the next day the story was published in the paper too— I found it at my father's and discreetly put it away for myself. To cut a long story short, originally some people were arrested for stealing from a farm—because there are suddenly an endless number of starvelings who take from others' produce without discrimination—and a couple of days beforehand, the authorities tried to shame them by marching them in the same way through the streets. However, the plan backfired, of course the town rabble started taking the thieves' side. Saying, what's wrong with that, can a person not glean the fields anymore, while the police turn a blind eye to the profiteering Jews?

By the next day, supposedly, the workers of the railway-engine repair shop were pushing for the sentencing of currency traffickers and black marketeers—and not in vain: according to the article, ten profiteering parasites were arrested. Although searches of their properties uncovered no foreign currencies, records referring to dollars were discovered, furthermore forty kilos of sugar, twenty kilos of laundry soap and thirty shirts were confiscated—railway workers meanwhile are forced to wear rags of course. Well, it was these very criminals I saw being escorted on a shame parade. Apparently, later on, the enraged underclass attacked the publicly humiliated Jews, whom the police barely managed to pull from the clutches of the hot-blooded protestors.

When the journalist questioned the necessity for this public shaming, the police superintendent answered that if they hadn't led these persons around the town, a pogrom would have broken out, the scale of which the Szolnok Jewry would not survive. Therefore, he believed that this action had taken the wind out of the anti-Semites' sails. The local leader of The Joint didn't agree, who believed there was no organized action at all being carried out to combat the palpable anti-Semitism in the county town. The rabble on the street, for example, would commonly hurl grave insults at the few Jews who were locally considered to be well off. Many even raised objections to The Joint offering free two-course lunches when only one was served to manual workers, and so it was declared: From here on in, it's one plate for everyone, Jews too.

*

At the Budapest trial, which I could watch from beginning to end, I was surprised to see the judge questioning policemen. He was interested in what the County Police superintendent might be able to say about the events in Kunvadas and so called out Nándor Gruber.

The testimony of the superintendent, who explained after questioning that he had joined the force upon returning from deportation and had served his post since the democratic restructuring of the police force, was roughly the following:

Honourable members of the Court, on the Tuesday in question the telephone rang at around half past two in the afternoon. The inspector of Karcag Constabulary made an unusually nervous phone call, shouting that there was serious trouble in Kunvadas and we should assist immediately. A pogrom broke out at the weekly market, he said, on account of the children sausages. Did he say children sausages?, I said to myself, what on earth is this man on about? But we go nonetheless. We were not armed and we were few, hence we took a roundabout route to gather our men. In the end, I utilized Sanyi Wágner's half-ton pickup and we set off with five or six policemen, two detectives and as many arms as we could manage.

When we arrived in the village, we saw that an angry crowd was gathering around the police station. Their clothes were bloody, their hands too. And acting like they were drunk. Shouting over one another that the Jews were butchering the children and chopping them up for sausage meat. All the while their own hands were dripping with blood. From what it seemed, they were the ones requesting protection, it didn't cross their minds that they might be arrested. Soon after, the Divisional Inspector and Second Lieutenant Brucker arrived with a typist, and the Russian *nachalnik* came—from the direction of the airstrip.

Here the judge started prying as to when exactly police had stood by idly while violent acts were being committed by the crowd.

The superintendent replied that it couldn't have happened long before their arrival to Kunvadas with reinforcements.

And then a sergeant was called forward who had admitted in the earlier investigation that he had watched as a defenceless person was beaten until dead. Ferenc Russ-Gross, yes. Another two constables were forced to corroborate. They now realize, they said, that their own pleading was unacceptable, namely, their pleading that they had not been given orders to act.

Efforts should have been made to avoid our transportation of casualties to the hospital, admitted the sergeant at last.

Those who were called on next were not being questioned for the first time. A woman compliantly stepped forward—I recognized her immediately.

The ninth-named defendant, please! Name, please?

Mrs Márton Vasvári.

I understand you were outraged by the news that Jews were murdering children?

Completely outraged, sir, I have five children of my own.

But then it turned out not a single child had gone missing, neither in Kunvadas nor in Karcag!

I didn't know that, sir, at the time.

Take a look at this photograph!

This one?

Yes, it shows two women holding cudgels. Can you identify yourself?

Myself . . . ?

Are you either of these women . . . ?

Just one of them . . .

Indeed, one of them is you. And not the person being beaten. But so who is the other?

Sára Tarcsai. My cousin.

Does she have a family?

Not her, no, just a child. She was left in that condition. Actually the father was killed in action . . .

And who is it you are beating?

Mrs György Weiner, seamstress.

Did you know her?

Of course. Her daughter was two years below me, Ica.

Now, read this out!

What's this?

I will ask the questions. However, it is the testimony of Sára Tarcsai, your cousin.

Why, where's Sára?

Read it!

So Mrs Vasvári set to it, and, in a drawling, stammering voice, she read: György Weiner lives close by with his wife and their daughter Ilona. They surely heard the commotion and shouting at the market. Or about our mood that morning. Their thinking was they would hide in the neighbour's attic without letting on to the owners. But we still found them. One of us had a shovel, a man, I don't know his name, he hit the Weiners in the back with that. Their daughter, Ica, ran down the attic steps, but the mother tripped and rolled the whole way down. She was wailing that she twisted her ankle. Her husband picked her up in his arms and hurried out to the street. Us behind them. And outside we saw that the shovel man and another one are chasing them and start hitting Weiner. And then they tie his hands together wanting to take him away. So Weiner's wife clings to her husband, they hit her in the head to knock her out and she falls in the ditch unconscious.

At this point the judge takes a sheet of paper from a file and begins reading from it: I came around to two women standing over my head on the bank of the ditch, contemplating whether I was alive or not. Then I moved to show I was alive and to ask them for a drink of water. And if they knew where my husband was. To which they say, Look, it's Mrs Weiner. The woman's still moving, she can take more beating.

That's not true, interrupted Mrs Vasvári. We didn't say she could take more beating.

But the judge wasn't interested, he carried on: And they started beating me wherever they could. They were Márton Vasvári's wife and Sára Tarcsai. I knew them. Fortunately at that point a policeman arrived with a Soviet officer, who chased away my attackers and had me taken to hospital.

Exactly!, said one of the Kunvadas policemen. Again it's clear there, sir, that we did intervene . . .

The judge carried on reading Mrs Weiner's statement: Four of my fingers were broken, and I received five stitches and seven stitches for the wounds on my head. My husband, György Weiner still hasn't regained consciousness from the concussion.

The judge set the paper down on the table. Well?, he looked to the policemen.

Well, yes, said the sergeant, pursing his lips. We . . . well, so . . . we were powerless. And he mentioned the example when the crowd were cramming into Gross the egg seller's yard, their first lieutenant's efforts to address the lynch mob were useless, the people wouldn't obey orders. So the officers drove off, they left Kunvadas. And didn't bother letting the constables know what to do with themselves.

Eventually, the judge heard the testimony of a young girl. He asked her age, eleven, and invited her to tell the court what she had seen.

There was an awful big crowd . . . the high street was crammed, one side to the other, with them coming . . . like a herd or something . . . I don't know where so many of them came from and where they went . . . And they were walking these Jews up at the front . . . Shoving them and hitting their backs. They went into their houses, chucked everything out the door and took it with them. They dragged out anyone they found inside. And they pulled the shopkeeper out of the wholesaler's onto the street and beat his head in, that's what I saw. Then I ran away, but I know, because people said, that it lasted the whole day.

*

I don't know which day of the trial it was when towards the evening a roughly sixty-year-old lady was led in who was in a dreadful state— and had evidently been forced to wait around since eight in the morning too. The judge took some time searching among his papers before asking her: Mrs Ferenc Neuberger?

The woman raised a tentative hand as if to correct him, and I too assumed some sort of mistake, because it couldn't be Mrs Neuberger whom I used to know well. Yet as she glanced around uneasily, I got a better look, and it occurred to me I had failed to recognize Mrs Neuberger once before, upon seeing her and her husband at the post office for the first time again after they had come back. I couldn't believe a person could age so much within mere months. Now I was mistaken a second time, it was absolutely Ágota

Neuberger Fehér, who was forty-five at most, but was now so sick and injured, completely broken, she had almost aged two decades.

Tears came to my eyes, I could barely focus on what she was saying. On the one hand, I realized that recently, when wondering whether I knew a single happily married couple, two people had failed to come to my mind. The Neubergers of course, but why on earth was I thinking about happiness . . . On the other hand, I recalled how as teenage girls, Anna Tószegi and myself had looked up to Ágota as a role model. Because she was not just a domestic wife next to Mr Neuberger, who owned the hardware shop, she was an equal, her husband's partner, she took over for him in the shop and had a knack for informing customers because she read up about the tools in German. She handled the business' correspondences and bookkeeping, was happy to offer advice, to give language tutorage, and she played the piano at house parties.

When I was sixteen my father sent me to Ágota's like to a school, to study commercial bookkeeping. No one has a better grasp than Mrs Neuberger, said Papa, and she knows how to explain it too. I was only willing to go if Anna Tószegi came too, but her father didn't want to spend money on that sort of thing. Finally, Ágota took us both on for the price of one student—if we're happier to learn together, then what does it matter. We visited her two afternoons a week for half a year, and the extensive syllabus included bookkeeping, a bit of statistics, handling business correspondence and even the fundamental phrases in German. In addition—outside of the lessons—she played us classical music records, recommended reading, trained our noses to recognize the difference between patchouli perfume and quality perfume, and had us both preparing tray bakes. On a couple of occasions, she and her husband took us with them to Karcag or Szolnok, once even to the theatre.

Well, isn't she kind, rejoiced my mother, very understandable though, because of course poor darling Ágota wasn't able to have children.

It never occurred to me that she didn't have any children. And how her husband still loves her!

I remember, as teenagers, Anna and I had several chats about why their kind provided us with the most appealing examples—because neither of us could deny that one day we wanted to live as Ágota did, and to love our partners as much as the Neubergers did—but we concluded that their kind also displayed the most repugnant qualities at the opposite pole. After all, it was among their breed we could observe the most repulsive behaviour—like boisterousness and overbearing nattering, sarcasm, bragging, and an innate penchant for deceiving others. And at their vilest stratum, we find the offence at being slighted or impoverished, the dark suspicion and the dishonesty—paired with the often-nauseating body features, not uncommonly crowned by slovenliness. In still worse cases, we might discover in them the commune rebel instinct, but even a potentially lethal, murderous anger lying dormant. Which could erupt if given the opportunity.

As we saw it, our well-considered classifications were overwhelmingly supported by years of first-hand experiences—and in a good sense too, because the classically appealing cases were just as typical as the more common bad examples. So when those well-known legislations were implemented against them, despairingly, Anna and I could list by name the great many people for whom our heart broke, because for them such treatment truly was inhumane, and for them an exception absolutely should be made. Maybe it's understandable as such why I thought it absolutely fair that Ágota Fehér and Ferenc Neuberger had escaped, and why I was so happy to see them again unharmed. But I was devastated I could no longer share any of this with my close friend Anna Tószegi, who died giving birth.

Come forward, please!, said the judge to Ágota. Go ahead! What is your name?

My name is Mr Ferenc Neuberger, and . . .

Cut the wisecracks!, snapped the judge at Ágota, but she wouldn't be swayed, and began the testimony in her husband's name again.

My name is Mr Ferenc Neuberger, and due to my own impediments I would like to state the following with my wife acting as intermediary. On the Tuesday in question, at ten o'clock in the morning on 21st May, our house was broken into. A hostile lynch mob toppled the gate, smashing it, then the kitchen door, to pieces. We intended to hide. They found us, pulled us out and interrogated us about a secret telephone. Supposedly, using said telephone we had alerted the police not to permit the crowd into the courthouse. We have never owned a telephone. We were shoved onto the street where they started beating both of us with wooden cudgels and scourges, shouting:

Is it a people's court you filth want? Here's your people's court! Think you can take our children? No more Jew rule!

Listening to Ágota, I was reminded of earlier that day, when half a dozen unkempt men and women of varying ages had lined up in the courtroom. They were asked whether they were members of the Kunvadas crowd that yelled anti-Semitic mottos, and to repeat the pogrom mottos for the court.

An expert answer was offered by the oldest witness, according to whom the pogrom's mottos were the following: No more Jew Courts! We'll be the judges now!

A young woman joined in: Christians united against Jew rule! Down with the Jews!

Down with the Communists!, said a man who looked like a worker, punching the air. Stand up to the Jews! Stop the kidnappers, protect out children! And all the rest, said the man, eventually lowering his arm.

Getting back to the lynching!, the judge turned to Mrs Neuberger, who was by now having difficulties standing. So it was with claim to the telephone that the crowd assaulted you and your husband. Were you injured?

I incurred the following injuries:

Which of you did?

Ferenc Neuberger. They were: a broken right arm, a broken rib, countless breaks and fractures around my head. But when the police wanted to transport my unconscious body, they were blocked by the crowd, who said a Jew can't be put on a Hungarian cart. In the later hours . . . six hours after being assaulted . . . sorry, no, seven hours after my assault, I, Ferenc Neuberger, died as a result of the injuries I had incurred. But I still heard one of the policemen curse, as he tripped over my wife lying on the ground, who, poor thing, was on her last legs. Kick this old bitch out of the way!, he said. Don't let me see her when she croaks!

I see, and you are . . . ?

Mrs Ferenc Neuberger!

So, finally . . . are or are you not deceased?

What do you think?

The judge looked away, ran a hand through his hair, and for the first time lost composure, maybe because even he was tired, so he quickly adjourned court.

*

Later, I heard several versions of the lynching that happened out at the airstrip, and given that all of the testimonies came from the culprits, people soon got down to guessing where the truth lay. Weeks after the disturbances, somebody had an investigating officer's interrogation records delivered to me, I can only refer to it alone—I'll add no comments of my own to the incident.

Who are you?, asked the investigating officer.

Kunvadas airstrip workers.

Tell us what form of abnormal event took place there on 21st May!

And straight away these witnesses—perhaps four of them— collectively, interrupting one another, tell the whole story until the end.

It was getting towards noon when a big group of people come out to us from the village. They said did we not fancy a little pogrom.

What programme?, we said.

Not a programme, a pogrom.

And what's that?

A sort of lynching, bit of a brawl . . .

Well . . . we said, might be interested . . . wouldn't say no. Us being airstrip labourers neither. But why are you asking, we said.

Because one of them was chased out here . . .

A whatchamacallit . . . an oven-dodger . . .

An itzer . . .

Never-got-to-Auschwitzer . . .

Would you stop . . . joking around?!, instructed the investigating officer, seemingly more grumbling than stern.

Anyway, this escapee was hiding here somewhere . . .

We need to flush him out . . . you know, to make a skirmish line.

All right, why not.

The airstrip workers needn't miss out, isn't that right lads?

We look up—was that not him stepping out from behind the wall?

It was.

About ten paces from us.

But who had stepped out from behind the wall?

The fella, the one they were following. The Rosenstein.

József Rosenstein, the soda man.

Where you off to, Jew?, we shouted.

Not scared you'll lose your jacket?, he was dangling it by his feet.

We were just looking for an excuse to pick a fight.

Why would I be scared of you?, he says.

Because we're Magyars, are we not!

Then him again with the same gall: A hundred Hungarians wouldn't scare him.

Tell you the truth, his wise-ass, haughty pompous guff wound us right the fuck up.

No cursing!, grumbled the officer. Understand?

So we surrounded him, but we were empty-handed. Then he got away, he flung himself past us and ran off.

What did you do?

Went after him.

And?

We hemmed him in, someone tripped him up, and he went to the ground.

We threw ourselves on him, he shoved two off, jumped to his feet, and it turned out that inside the coat he was carrying a branch of cornel wood. He wielded the stick with such a wild face, we didn't dare go for him.

That's when I made an unexpected appearance on the scene; József Konya, fifth-named defendant. I walked up to the stocky Rosenstein and tore the weapon from his hands. Then one of the labourers punched him on the chin so hard he keeled over. And then we all started hitting him. Some just using their bare hands or a stretch of cable, but most of us taking turns to beat Rosenstein with the branch of cornel wood we'd ripped from his hands, we dealt blows to every inch of the injured party's body. And then some of us left, while Rosenstein was still alive, in fact, he stood up from the ground. Three of us went over to him again and beat him some more with the branch in question, until the branch snapped. That's when I left.

But by that point the injured party was no longer alive, correct?, asked the officer.

He would have been fine, except Ferenc Ugari, the juvenile defendant, he hit him with a stone. Later we heard that from his injuries incurred during the assault, the injured party died on the spot, within minutes.

I saw the body while on police duty. I remember Rosenstein's bloody face, his reddish moustache, his torn clothes. At the top left part of his head, behind his ear, there was a fist-sized, oval, brownish stone sticking out. I touched him but he didn't move. He had been struck hard and from up close by someone, we still don't know who. The poor Jew was stoned to death. He died a biblical death.

*

A long time had passed since the summary hearing in Szolnok was adjourned, when Irén Gellért suddenly responded to my letter. Regrettably, she wrote, she only just heard from her husband that our trial was adjourned, and she was glad we could be relieved for the time being. She informed me furthermore that an old comrade of her husband's put him forward for the Miskolc City Communist Party Committee, and at his new work, Ferrie had been immediately thrown in at the deep end, he was already being delegated rather important tasks. Before she signed off, Irén made an apology, the postman still didn't know them in the new place, and sadly my letter was delivered to them late, but that we must return to its subject soon (namely, that they testify in my husband's trial) whenever we get a chance to speak in person. She was making preparations to visit her mother in Kunvadas one weekend, to let little Laci visit his grandmother, and perhaps we could meet then.

*

More than once I have wondered whether we could have altered the events, whether we could have done something differently on that dire 21st May—or the day before, on the Monday. But I don't see what we could and should have done substantially differently which could have prevented the developments from occurring, or which would have been more appropriate merely from the perspective of our self-defence.

There is one exception which I think did prove to be a mistake—even if we weren't at fault personally, after all it hadn't been my husband's idea—and that was the cross-party meeting arranged on the evening of the pogrom. The onus of which must have lain heavy on Gergely Kátai's conscience. But given that Sándor and Gergely were not merely friends but fellow victims of the same ordeal, we too had to bear the consequences of this event. Presumably, in the background of Kátai's unfortunate initiative there must have been some intention to clarify, or even to shift responsibility, but once it was over, after what happened, none of us knew where it would lead.

I don't remember precisely but it must have been four or half past five when I escorted old Mr Gold, just regaining his senses beside the ditch, and his wife, into their house. Outside it looked as if the dirty tide of lynching was subsiding, so I left them alone. But I could barely walk among the heaps of rubbish and the ruins left in the wake of the destruction, the shards of glass cracked beneath my feet, while I made my way home cutting across the slowly emptying main street. Unlocking the gate and doors, I began calling Sándor's name from the garden, asking where he was, but couldn't find him anywhere, until I noticed the note on the table. He had to go over to Gergely Kátai's to discuss something, but I wasn't to worry, he would be back soon.

But indeed I was worried, in fact I was terrified. I don't think these two want to be putting their heads together right now, I say, they shouldn't be contributing any ideas at all. I felt as though I couldn't let them handle matters themselves, because they might exacerbate the already catastrophic situation.

I hurried to the Kátais' house but didn't find the two friends there, just Gergely Kátai's frail mother, who knew nothing and said to try the Smallholders' office. But on the way there, someone said there was a meeting in the town hall, they had seen the men going in. I would have ran straight away, but at that moment Etel Radai's gang appeared up ahead, so I hid in the privy and had to waste half an hour.

When I arrived, a shock trooper in an R-Guard armband blocked my path and said only people sent by a party could enter. I was, I said. Who are you? The women's section of the Smallholders Party, without flinching I gave him my name, he wrote it down, I could go.

There must have been fifty people inside, all talking at once, and the person chairing—one of Kátai's men, it seemed—appeared callow, he couldn't keep order. The moment someone started talking about where such-and-such atrocity took place, others immediately interrogated the speaker, asking whom they were representing and on what grounds.

The cross-party meeting will continue its work as follows, said the chairman, we shall put forward an agenda—a hand went up, and grocer Andor Reményi stood:

May I add a few words?

From your party?, pouted Kátai, ignoring the chairman, and nodded, Okay, but keep it brief, please.

Very brief, nodded Reményi. As regards the comments of the local Jews who incurred the injuries . . . First of all: the pogrom was organized in advance by certain instigators. This is proven by the fact the telephone lines were cut and the roads leading out of the village were blocked . . .

Reményi couldn't speak any further, heckles rained down on him:

Lies! The telephones were working!

Only a few lines were cut. Towards the end.

The roads . . . ? What do you . . . ?

Impossible . . . ! Who would even . . . ?!

Further evidence the pogrom was organized, said Andor Reményi, trying to continue, the blocked roads meant the railway workers were waiting in ambush for József Rosenstein, who was fleeing along the tracks, and beat him to death.

The railway workers have nothing to do with it! Insisted Kátai's brother, Márton, vehemently, while one of his pals added that anyway Rosenstein fled towards the airstrip.

Supposedly he wasn't so much fleeing as attacking.

But he cocked it up. Shouldn't have acted Jack the Lad.

Quiet, please!, the chairman hammered the table. Quiet! I call on Gergely Kátai, secretary of the Kunvadas Smallholders, at whose initiative this meeting was held. Over to you!

Thank you, said Kátai, remaining in his seat. This day marks a sad turning point in the life of our small town, but it also shines some light on certain consistencies. I suggest therefore that two things be put on record. The first: the cross-party meeting regrets the events that have taken place, expresses its sympathy—et cetera, et cetera, as decency requires. The second: The meeting hereby calls on every Kunvadas citizen of Jewish descent, whose presence in our town evidently will never cease to stir up . . .

Stir up . . . ?!, snapped an unfamiliar woman in a blue cardigan. stir up what?!

Unrest, said Kátai. Yes, what's so astonishing about that . . . ?

What do you mean by . . . ?

Kátai, paying no attention to the person interrupting, went on: Namely, since their residence here poses an obstacle for peace in the town, as soon as possible . . . no—within six hours, they are requested to relocate to another locality.

Hear, hear!, someone agreed, and many more joined in:

Just right! Finally . . . !

Finally someone says the truth, it's high fucking time we talked about it . . . !

Time we talked about the real reason!

Gergely! At last I brought myself to speak, took a deep breath, stood up and shouted, Gergely Kátai, do you really want to drive them out? You can't say a thing like that! I looked around in shock, because nobody paid me any attention, Kátai himself seemed not to hear, he stared at me, as though puzzling over what I meant to say. At first I thought they hadn't understood what I was saying over the racket, so I shouted a few more words, but then realized, they were making a din because they understood precisely what I was saying, they just didn't like it. Only now did I notice my husband among the shoulders jostling behind Gergely, I could read from Sándor's face he was confused about what I wanted to say, and signalled to elbow over to him, but I didn't care to.

The woman in the blue cardigan, however, had now managed to shout down the yea-sayers and was attacking Gergely ferociously: This is absurd! Kátai, you seem to think you're at a meeting for Béla Imrédy's party?!

What party are you talking about?, asked Kátai, bewildered.

You know very well what party. Your own far-right racist party!

That's a lie. I was never a member of that party.

I've no idea whether you had a membership or not, she shrugged. But you certainly hung about with them.

You're mixing me up with someone else. Or, to put it less kindly, that's just plain slander.

Kátai! At the time you were walking and talking exactly like the rest of them who . . .

All right, we've enough of this woman's slanders, I say to myself, my husband will be the next name she calls out, so we shout her down. Everyone shouts something different:

Be quiet . . . !

Don't get your knickers in a twist!

What are you squawking on about?

Furthermore, sorry to say, but anyone so biased, who is affected due to their descent, ought not to . . .

And then several people kept repeating—with which of course I didn't agree—that it was well known that throughout the village, the grand majority were of the same opinion as Gergely Kátai.

Hear, hear! Any people who can't live in peace can pack up and leave!

The troubles are all because of them!

There are rules to living together in one society!

That's right! There are rules!, Gergely's brother, Márton, sprang up. And that's exactly why we support their resettlement outside of our town, before . . .

Before it gets any worse? The cardigan lady was shouting over the top of everyone. Is that right?, she screamed, shrilly. Before it gets any worse than today . . . ?! Is that right . . . ?!

Oh, now, come on, come on, come on!, a stout, fast-talking lady stood—a representative of the Women's Association, someone said beside me. The things that have been said in this room, honourable colleagues!, began her sympathetically chastising complaint. Expelling all Jews without discrimination? It makes no sense. And those days have been and gone. Sorry, sorry, before anyone drowns me out . . . My husband is Jewish. To that extent I am affected too. You don't need to tell me. However, I understand . . . can I finish?, she looked reproachfully at those shouting over her, however, I understand that the majority are of the view that in the village there are many Jews who in certain regards are the cause . . . Because of whom recurrent anti-Semitic sentiments are falling on the heads of innocent people, innocent Jews. I suggest a compromise. Therefore . . .

OK. Let's cut the speeches!, Gergely Kátai interrupted the Women's Association lady, he stood and, as usual, pulled an unwarranted smile. If everyone agrees, then we'll put the following on record: The cross-party meeting first request that the Communist Party Secretary Ferenc Hámos and his wife leave the village.

My husband was the first to speak: The Hámoses?, he asked, and was shocked. Why pick the Hámoses, Gergely, of all people?

And of all people, you're asking, Sándor?, retorted Kátai and continued dictating. Furthermore, we demand that those among the Jewish population of Kunvadas who willingly refuse to integrate into the democratic life of the village leave the settlement, in their own interest, because no political party can espouse responsibility for their safety.

Can espouse responsibility . . . , repeated the shorthand, Like this—espouse?

Do we accept this proposal?, the chairman raised the question, and had us vote. The hands rose, I was paralysed and had stopped shouting too. As I see it, said the chairman without counting, the majority are in support.

We, however, do not accept the proposal, stood up the man in the suit, whose arm was in a sling.

Who are you?, asked the chairman, at which an introduction followed, peppered with jeers and taunts. Apparently, two of them were representing the local Social Democrats at the bedridden Károly Würczel's request, while the two Communists must have been delegated by Ferenc Hámos, whom the organizers refused to invite to this meeting, or the two came against Hámos' will, nobody knew which was the case. All four declared that after all that has been said, as left-wing representatives they aren't willing to give any explicit reason why they refuse to sign this appeal concerning Jews and demanding they leave the village. But they request that their opposition be recorded.

Your opinion will be added, said the chairman, looking to the shorthand, who nodded. Your insignificant minority opinion.

Excuse me—sorry, what's your name?—why is your arm in a sling?, Gergely Kátai asked the Communist in the suit.

Because he was a victim, retorted Andor Reményi the grocer on the other's behalf, The lynchers attacked him, and his name is Antal Juhász.

So you were attacked as a Jew?

Yes, the anti-Semitic rabble dislocated his arm!, affirmed Reményi a second time.

Is that true, Juhász?, Kátai walked over to the injured man, who stammered that it was true, though he felt he wasn't attacked as a Jew but as a Communist.

160

Evidently because you're not a Jew, are you, continued Kátai, and told the room that he heard a completely different story. In fact, he heard that Juhász was just about to flee the violence on the street when among the murderers attacking the Neubergers and breaking into their house, he suddenly recognized his own Communist Party cell in full attendance. And when he called to them from the gateway to ask what they were doing, they set upon him, gave him a good old clobbering and chased him on his way. Isn't that right?

No, sir . . . not in . . . they weren't in full attendance, stammered Juhász, and Reményi repeated, you cannot deny this man gave resistance to the lynchers.

The chairman then called for silence, saying that he just received a note bearing another person's request to speak. Please, can we have silence for the delegates of the Communist Party from Budapest?

A bureaucrat wearing glasses stood up. Thank you. Firstly: since our arrival from Budapest, the police have continuously refused to illuminate us as liaisons of the Hungarian Communist Party by any means whatsoever. On the contrary, we were warned not to speak with the locals, as there was, I quote, no need to stir up the public mood. Therefore, I would first like to strongly request the same of the gentleman who spoke before me, he fixed his gaze on Gergely Kátai. It would very much be in his own interest to refrain from any unnecessary and deceitful stirring-up of the public mood.

What's so deceitful?, muttered Gergely's brother, Márton.

So, if I may, said this sly piece of work, removing his notes. One can ascertain that what happened here is the consequence of a so-called recurrent anti-Semitism, one which has infected the entire area. The authorities are reluctant to hold the war criminals to account, who conversely present themselves as martyrs and lure the local population towards their own sides. Anti-Jewish incitement being the simplest and, among primitive minds, most opportune means available. Almost eight hundred people took part in the pogrom. Several thousand, however, idly stood by, until the very end, and there was not a single person among them willing to make any attempt to stem the tide of lynching.

But that's exactly what our comrade did!, Reményi pointed to the man in the sling.

And there was another exception, a woman in the audience stood up, before continuing: The wife of Ferenc Bujdosó, my sister-in-law, our Bözsi, who was beaten for coming to the defence of two Jews who were being attacked. Of course, I thought, this must be the Bözsi who was born a Jew. But this had since escaped public knowledge, only I remembered.

May I continue?, the Communist liaison asked impatiently. What could be more typical of the previously illustrated infection than that at the county court today once again, a huge tumult gathered for the trial of the Catholic priest, who faces charges of fascism and praising Ferenc Szálasi, leader of the Arrow Cross. At the crowd's demand, the hearing was relocated to the courthouse yard, where at least five hundred people were in an uproar. Allow me to quote what was heard:

Come on Jews! Accuse us if you dare! We're here now, try telling us now! We'll never abandon our minister! We came to drink Jew blood! The Jews are on trial now, and we're the judges! Kill the vermin Jews!

And so on and so forth. And even though the police force was present, you see, there was still nothing that could be done, the hearing had to be postponed. While the accused priest remains at liberty!

Because he's innocent!, interrupted Gergely Kátai.

What a load of crap!, added Gergely's brother, Márton. Why would he not be at liberty?!

If I'm not mistaken, it is still my turn to speak, remarked the liaison curtly. Furthermore, returning to the matter at hand. Those who were arrested after the Kunvadas pogrom were almost exclusively juveniles and Gypsies.

Again the heckles were pelted at him thick and fast:

So what?

What's wrong with that?

Is it not criminals you're after . . . ?

Who do you want?

However!, and he raised his finger. Spared from custody were the masterminds and leaders of the incident!

Who walk free though their identities are known to the police, remarked a downy, barely fledged young man standing behind the liaison.

Who are you implying?

The people who were active in organizing these disturbances, replied the fuzzy lad. Besides Sándor Hadnagy the schoolmaster and his wife, Dr Dezső Császár of the Peasant's Party, for example, János Cseh the minister, and Gergely Kátai the Smallholders secretary.

Is he talking about me?, Gergely looked at Sándor.

And me, said Sándor.

If those are your names, nodded the scoundrel, then yes, you.

At that moment, thank God, all hell broke loose in the room and the best part of the crowd took our side.

Lies!

Demented finger pointing!

Slander!

We demand a proper enquiry!

Filthy liars!

I will stand before any enquiry, said my husband, as he stepped forward with the greatest calm. And I will say now that the entire village, including Communist Party Secretary Hámos, will testify to the fact that I, Sándor Hadnagy, did not put a single foot outside of my house once, precisely so that I could not be smeared as an instigator. And nor did the rest of the listed members of the village's intelligentsia. We are innocent. We were in our homes. It is true, however, as a result, sadly nobody was there to defuse the enraged mob.

The Communist liaison reeled off a statement that investigations would be carried out concerning people's whereabouts at various times, their activity, and their inactivity.

Something has already been confirmed!, the liaison suddenly thrust a finger into the air, Mr Hadnagy has just admitted that none of you made any attempt to suppress the pogrom. We know that the very instant the fighting broke out at the market, landowner Gergely Kátai, teacher Sándor Hadnagy, the lawyer and the doctor all vanished into thin air. The Calvinist minister also failed to act, who during his sermons in previous days hadn't even mentioned the blood libel hysteria.

The chairman introduced a newly arrived guest and invited him to speak: County Police Superintendent Nándor Gruber would like to give a statement.

The police superintendent, who by his own quick admission was directly affected due to his racial background, emphasized that, unfortunately, no one could have intervened in the pogrom. Hence the telegram sent from Kunvadas, he says, to the National Office of Israelites, and forwarded directly to Prime Minister Ferenc Nagy. Who sent it to Minister of the Interior László Rajk, from whom we got the following order, said Superintendent Gruber, producing the slip from his pocket:

I have ordered the investigation begin immediately. Swift retaliation crucial towards reassuring society and foreign opinion. Signed: Rajk

When the meeting was over, I quickly exited the main hall and, pausing by the ground floor banisters to wait for Sándor, I had an awkward encounter. Irén Hámos came speeding down, almost knocking me over, of course I had to say hello.

She stopped, returned my greeting, and I said uncomfortably: So you attended the meeting, did you, Irén? I didn't see you.

She listened to the whole thing from the gallery, she replied, and it had clearly shaken her. We weren't to worry, she said, visibly upset, our request would be granted, her husband and she were leaving the village as fast as possible.

But I think it's completely unjust, you know I said so, publicly.

You did, but your husband . . .

He was scandalized too.

Scandalized? But he still went and voted for his old pal Kátai's idea.

And she turned on her heel, but stopping in the doorway, said this wasn't what I promised when I visited in the afternoon. I didn't call after her, but she wouldn't have listened.

I deliberately didn't tell a word of this exchange to Sándor when he arrived, there's time, I say to myself, I'll tell him later. I remember, as we were leaving for home, at first we were frightened by the extreme allegations made by the Communists from Budapest. We reassured each other that the grounds were so preposterous, the accusation would never hold up, then forgetting our initial fright, by the time we got home we were in a heated argument.

Because Gergely Kátai was an idiot to make a confused, hasty call for this cross-party meeting when he plainly had not thought through what on earth he wanted from it. Since anyone could see the whole performance would do more harm than good, Sándor would do better in such situations to warn his friend, who, lacking any real self-confidence, is forever using that irritating, unnecessary smirk, to escape shooting himself square in the foot.

My husband truly didn't understand who or what this gathering might have harmed—the Communists' insults notwithstanding, which would have come out one way or another.

I'm scared, most of all for you two, I answered, because you publicly laid your cards on the table, for what, I do not know. I told him how unseemly I found it, that at the meeting not only were certain viewpoints tolerated but also that Kátai even had them pushed through in a vote. So it gave the appearance the Smallholders intended to mete out their own justice and sentences, and were forestalling the results of an investigation.

Frankly, I explained this to my husband much too generously, because in reality these were not mere appearances and intentions. But Sándor still denied it, he didn't think our party's members were trying to forestall any investigation, consequently they couldn't deliver judgements, and in fact it was the left-wingers who deserved such blame.

True, I said, but right now I'm not thinking about who carried out the lynchings. Rather, it's no use to either of you for any investigation to conclude that certain people have to leave the village because their presence gives rise to unrest.

But that's not what he supported. The proposition that would have applied to everyone without discrimination, said Sándor, was extreme for him too. Besides, he stood up for the Hámoses when they were singled out.

You stood up and sat straight back down, I said. Unfortunately, it just so happens I did the same.

He doesn't think there was anything else we could have done in all that commotion.

Sándor, sweetheart, I said, shaking my head, deep down one might wish half the village were banished, but it's not a thought worth sharing. Now, Gergely has brought accusations against himself and against you I'm afraid. You both voted for this stupid nonsense. You would send off the Jews that were unwilling to integrate on the very day a bloody pogrom is carried out against them—but not the lynchers?

Nobody was defending the lynchers, he said. Their role should be investigated and they should answer for their actions. But why not relieve tensions from both sides?, he insisted. And explained that he, like Gergely, was trying to broaden his perspective, to look at this whole situation from all sides, not just one.

Eventually—as we were going to bed—he was talking about how, to this day, he still believes that the truth must always be added up collectively, because it never hides in one corner. Which is why he's confident the right thing to do is to confront debates head-on rather than stifle them, it's more honourable to stand by your views than to hide them under a bushel. And he isn't saying it out of a lack of modesty, because he's never been a man for bragging, but still today in his own quiet way he didn't take fright at his attackers, he squarely met their allegations without blinking, shrugged off their calumnies, and calmly said to their faces that he would stand before an investigation. And of course he doesn't expect any sort of special recognition, but he does want me to know that in these moments, it isn't the cadets' or the village's opinions he means to impress, it's only ever my own.

Hearing this confession from him while staring into his eyes, every inch of me unexpectedly began to melt, until a minute later desires were flowing down my abdomen and up my thighs, the likes of which I hadn't experienced in years. I grabbed my husband's wrist with both hands, who was struck by the electric current, wasn't half glad and didn't delay. Without making any fuss, he tore off what wasn't necessary and held me so close I couldn't breathe. But in that moment, when he lay me on my back, a thought seemed to flash not into my mind but between my clenching, closing thighs, that only a few hours ago, somebody again violently attempted a similar act with me, I immediately froze, and started to tremble. Sándor patiently made his best effort to soften me and warm me, but for nothing, and so, as per our usual routine, he relieved himself against my hip.

*

I spent a good part of July 1946 in Budapest—I stayed with the usual lady at Kálvin Square. The people's court hearing had arrived, when I sat through every single day of my husband's trial for over three weeks. Though I took great pains to pay attention, I made very few notes. Thinking back on the period, I chiefly remember women, because the lion's share of the defendants in the dock were women, typically filthy, stinky, barefooted, raggedy, dim-witted women, with terror in their eyes.

Most of all, I wanted to see Sándor, so every day I tried to choose a place among the benches, where at least we could nod to one another, and send glances, since we were forbidden to write letters.

I imagined that by the time he came home I would have heaps of notes to show him. Though, I didn't know if he would be pleased that I wrote down the details of what I experienced in the village on the day of the disturbances. Perhaps I ought to keep those pages separately, I thought.

*

I travelled home for the first weekend, because there weren't any hearings on Saturday and Sunday, but came back on Friday evening after dark to avoid notice. I wanted to keep distant from my parents' interrogations, mother's hand-wringing, father's superciliousness, I didn't feel I had the strength to play the part of the dauntlessly optimistic wife. I was shattered, though I had spent the entire week sitting—on courtroom benches, in the guesthouse, on the train— constantly waiting. Now I wanted to sleep, to be alone, to not be paying attention. Hence I decided not to visit my parents' until Sunday lunch, when I would pretend I had just arrived, and only had a couple of hours in the village.

Therefore, I wasn't at all happy to find Mrs Hámos' letter in the post, in which Irén simply wrote she wanted to call by the next day. She has plans to travel home to Kunvadas anyway, she wants to see how her mother is getting on, and maybe, on Saturday afternoon we could have a chat, if I liked.

Well, I don't!, what do I have to talk about with her? And all this letter writing—what's the sense in it?! But to be fair, she didn't paint me with the same brush as the villagers who drove them out, instead she called by my house and sympathized with my problem, I recognize that. And since I was clutching at straws in my desperation, I wrote to her—but what good did it do?

Meanwhile, no matter which way I look at things, ultimately Hámos is the reason for everything that happened.

He had already been making jibes at Sándor back during the land redistribution!, I suddenly remembered. Because in May of '45, when my husband went to observe the parcelling-out to make sure they didn't touch the schoolmasters' endowments, Ferenc Hámos started by saying:

So, do tell, Mr Hadnagy! Which wild pear tree did you have in mind?

Sándor had no idea what he was talking about. Well, said Hámos, I'm talking about the message sent by the landowners to the Communists who are dividing up land for the destitute. I'm neither of the above, my husband shrugged, I have land but no more than is due to a schoolmaster. Meanwhile, two-thirds of the village has damn all!, retorted the others. What could he say, it was regrettable. But what was this message?

The message was, replied Ferenc Hámos, glowering, that if us Communists take what belongs to someone else, we'll be strung up from the nearest wild pear tree. That's the sort of message your people are sending.

At which Sándor chuckled, but said nothing more to the swaggering land-distribution committee, just dismissed them with a wave of the hand and left.

And then came their slander about the Levente cadets. If Hámos' people hadn't reported my husband with allegations of circulating war propaganda and endangering the youth, then there would have been no Karcag trial and nothing to protest. And if they hadn't stirred up unrest in people, the rabble wouldn't have started rioting, or rather lynching, and now my husband wouldn't be facing charges brought against him by summary or people's courts filled with more of Ferenc Hámos' ilk.

So Mrs Hámos needn't come to me to whine. Even if nobody else will so much as look at me—especially now I've become the wife of a jailbird. My husband's innocence is of no importance to people, who haven't a clue, they just warily sniff at the air and smell that I stink, that they had best keep their distance.

The next day I slept a lot, not knowing what to do with myself, I flicked through my notes but wrote nothing new. Eventually I took out the last novel I was reading which I had stopped halfway, *The Second Love* by Ferenc Herczeg, and got lost in it for hours. Later, when I heard Mrs Hámos' knocking, I remained in my seat. I didn't answer.

And then the day after, whom do I bump into while changing trains at Füzesabony Station? Irén! Oh, perhaps I had noticed a familiar chestnut-brown suit in the crowd earlier! But I say nothing. Straight away she laughs, Dearie me, did us two miss each other! She visited my house but nobody was home. Ah, I say, afraid not, and now I'm headed for Budapest, and she for Miskolc in the opposite direction.

But we've half an hour at least, she says, let's sit, there's something I want to tell you, Mária. Well, I think, how come this woman's being so familiar? And I remembered what was odd about her letter—that she opened and closed in a formal manner, but halfway got distracted and was as familiar as a close friend.

So she doesn't know the latest about my husband's trial, but she has been following it in the papers and the story has been preying on her mind. Because the pogrom didn't happen quite how it's being reported.

Which bit? I ask.

Well, that your husband was allegedly a ringleader.

So you two wouldn't agree that my husband was the ringleader of a pogrom? I said, to which she replied, she understands my bitterness and why I mock her, but there's more. She means he didn't even participate. Everyone she has spoken to agrees. It would help a great deal, I replied, if she told that to the court too.

That's just why she wanted to talk to me. Because she's been debating this for weeks with her husband. And Ferrie initially wouldn't hear a word about testifying, but when the defendants were brought before a summary court she started pleading with Ferrie, who wavered after all. And started believing her that neither Sándor Hadnagy nor Gergely Kátai accused the Jews of infanticide and incited the rabble to launch an anti-Semitic pogrom or to lynch the left-wing citizens. But think about it, she says, how and to whom could she and Ferrie have testified? Before the Szolnok trial there had been a window of only two or three days, what's more, travelling from Miskolc . . . ! And then fortunately news came that the summary court was suspended.

Ever since, she makes her husband read all the papers, and he admits the articles are exaggerated. But the debate of what to do in their situation hasn't been resolved. Should one testify to not having seen so-and-so at the time of their alleged crime? The person could have done it regardless of whether I saw them or not. Especially if I never left the house—how would I have seen anyone? That's Ferrie's stubborn position and, admittedly, it's true.

OK, but you admit, I say to him, continues Mrs Hámos, that these charges are horrific, we have to do something.

Well, he can't. And what's more, he says, am I to testify for the very same people who chased us from the village?

Ferrie, you're right, I say, but be honest, you weren't so sorry to leave and neither was I. You're enjoying the move and your new position more than you would our honeymoon I suspect, which by the way we still have not taken. Besides, your nerves were shattered in that dusty hole from the rivalry with Würczel and the Social Democrats, and clashes with your own party, for that matter. Not to mention the rest of it. You don't mind me, Mária, talking about our village in this way?

OK, that's true, said Ferrie, but he's got no time to deal with this now, because in Miskolc he's been lumped with organizing worker dissatisfaction and the fight for the new forint.

So that's how things stood, Irén continued, until two weeks ago when I gave him an ultimatum because it weighed on my heart. I said to him, Ferrie, dear, I've just read that the Budapest trial of Sándor Hadnagy's people is starting, I'm going to the city and I'm testifying, with or without you.

And he forbade me. At first he tried to justify it, saying I wouldn't be able to verify an alibi for your husband's people, but I was adamant and finally he revealed, almost in tears, why there could be no word of testifying. Because within the party he had to promise that he and his family would pledge themselves to never engage in any issue on their own authority. And since his special assignments are bound to this covenant, his lips are sealed, but I must understand that what I'm asking for is impossible.

I had to tell you this, my dear, said Irén, taking my hand, because my conscience would have troubled me so, had I not.

I sat bewildered and dumbfounded—on tenterhooks too because I had to keep an eye on the clock, I should have been waiting on the platform if I wanted to get a seat when the train arrived— and I weighed up what we were losing, what use Irén Hámos might have been to us in the trial. Nothing, none, I realized, it's not the participation of Sándor and his people in the lynchings we need to refute—the judge knows full well they didn't take part. All that interests the judge is whether or not they were inciters, or at least harboured hostile sentiments. And in those terms it's better if Irén keeps quiet.

Hence, I gave no response but a squeeze of her hand. Thank you, Irén, but I have to run. I waved to her and left.

*

I was continually racked with some form of guilt because I had no means at all to influence the lawsuit, so it appeared as though I was just allowing whatever would happen to happen. And this feeling troubled me. But if I am powerless, I tell myself, the least I can do is give it my full attention, properly follow the entire suit. Yet that too proved unsuccessful, I couldn't always keep track of the hearing's proceedings. My defence was that of course I couldn't because in the courtroom I constantly stare at Sándor, so memories flood back, all kinds of thoughts flash into my mind. Both serious and everyday things, like whether he's able to get any cigarettes. Or I look out for moments we can communicate with each other, I can't pay attention to anything else. But that's only partly true. The other cause for my absent-mindedness was cowardice, pure and simple—somewhere subconsciously I suspected the worst and didn't have the courage to confront it. I was girlishly covering my eyes and ears so I wouldn't be a witness if some horror were truly underway.

On the eve of the judgement's delivery, I was shocked by my own behaviour, pressing Sándor's lavender-scented handkerchief to my nose and talking to myself—because who else was there? I didn't want to confide in my landlady and my father had only arrived one or two days prior, who anyway seemed to think me non compos mentis. So I asked myself, having sat through the entire trial, what I thought the judge's verdict would be tomorrow. I was totally unable—or didn't dare—to give an answer. Instead I said, no matter how accurately or inaccurately we guess, a few hours later it won't matter anyway. Because our imminent, anxiously awaited judgement is unclear to everyone, nobody can foresee the end. Today, I wouldn't say that nobody foresaw what was to come. At most, I'd say—though not unsuspecting—I was blind. That much is certain.

That is to say, the next day, on 25th July, my husband was sentenced to death. And Gergely Kátai too. So was Zsigmond Rácz, that rabble-rousing scut, but I won't get into that. Vainly, from the moment I saw the first lynched victim, I had known what was in store, and against which we would have to defend ourselves, with all our might. Yet we failed, on this day our fight slumped to defeat. Such shameful disgracing of the law seemed impossible. And what was I to do now, I didn't know.

*

For days I wasn't all together. My father stirred sedatives into my drinks and told me not to believe the news. I mustn't believe it because it won't happen, we immediately filed an appeal. And if my acquaintance in the parliament believes the case is mostly political, explained my father, then as the largest party, the Smallholders, for the sake of their own prestige, cannot allow the violent left wing to demonstrate their efficiency in seizing power at the cost of the blood of innocent men.

But the fact that a judge would disregard both Sándor's and Gergely's perfect alibis for that whole day? That they could be principals without even being present?! It was inconceivable. Of course, in hindsight I now recognize that personal presence and actual participation were of no interest to the judge, merely the alleged incitement and organization as masterminds. Which he believed could have occurred earlier and from within the house.

I still couldn't speak to Sándor—though Papa thought it wouldn't be good for my husband to see me in such a state—but I was told I could write him a letter and was promised he would receive it. I gathered my strength and wrote him the same encouraging words I heard from my father. I phrased it carefully, so that from my words my husband would read a loving, reassuring hug, without suspecting I could be saying goodbye. The next day we left Budapest to go home to Kunvadas.

*

Before boarding the train, Papa and I heard that at the National Assembly there was a great deal of uproar about the sentences. The Smallholders spoke of a political attack because the judge unequivocally linked the Kunvadas men who received the death sentence with the Smallholders Party. Why do you fail to mention the summary trial in Szolnok which was adjourned, levelled one Smallholder parliamentarian at the left, where all eight principal suspects were members of the Communist Party's own rabble—excluding only those slandered with incitement—they even addressed each other as comrade during the summary court, and so the whole proceeding had to be immediately suspended!

My parents got wind from my father's acquaintance, the MP, that more than likely, after this kind of sentence, the case would be sent up for review to the National Council of the People's Courts. God almighty, I hope it brings some good!, Mama and I sighed.

When I got home, finally alone, I collapsed onto Sándor's daybed and let the pain flood through me. At first I wondered how long this would last—presumably as long as my own solitude—but didn't bear to dwell on what would come of me were it to last forever. Later I increasingly felt it would make no difference whether I gave in to despair or strove on optimistically, because regardless of my own determination, I would be seized by fear and loneliness forever.

After some hours, when I came around, it occurred to me I might look for my husband's letters written during the re-annexation of Transylvania and his postcards sent from the front—we had never really exchanged love letters because in those days we lived in the same neighbourhood and were never apart. Yet as I read I was now disappointed. To my memory, at the time, Sándor's sentences had aroused more passionate emotions in me—naturally because each time I was relieved he was alive and well—but he was never what you might call a witty stylist.

Later, I opened the wardrobes, and along the window side of our made bed, I laid his shirts, underwear, suits and hats, then the winter coat, the fur kalpak, the raincoat, and at the end of the bed his shoes and boots. I turned down the bed for myself, leaving Sándor's clothes on his side. The widow's bed, my Mezőkövesd grandmother's name for her half-made bed suddenly flashed into my mind, and terrified me. It wouldn't do to seek comfort for the pain of someone lost and gone, rather, I have to think of him as being alive and present—so I got out of bed to hold his clothes tight, to breathe in their smoky musk and the lavender scent of his handkerchiefs.

*

The next day a new letter came from Irén. She was devastated by the judgement she had read in the newspaper, and so, dismayed, again shared her compassion and insisted I was not to lose hope, it was still appealable, it couldn't end at that. But while she wrote about hope and made promises we would soon be able to speak in person about what I could do in my situation, there was an air of desperation in her letter. Especially once I turned the page.

Because that was not the only content of Irén's letter. Unexpectedly, on a new page, she wrote that as a friend of the same village, I would surely understand what she and her husband felt one day when in their new neighbourhood the same horror appeared on their doorstep as they had just fled.

According to Irén, our own tragedy in Kunvadas had been a harbinger to this newer case, which happened on 30th July in Miskolc, the city where they had been living a mere month and a half. And alas, fate may well have spared her from coming face to face with the lynchings in Kunvadas—albeit behind locked doors, petrified that the vandal horde would soon come for their lives— here, however, the same muddy wave of frightful rabble reached them too. She and her husband were on the street—they weren't put in any danger, luckily, but the whole thing happened before their eyes and there was nothing they could do.

An unpredictable, erratic throng bands together and starts sounding off, that ironworkers earned a decent wage before the war, but now they get less than a farmhand, in worthless money too, and they curse the bloody reactionaries and exploiters. We've barely two fillér to rub together, we're hungry, they shout, we have to barter for a bite of food, and that's if we have anything worth trading for.

The Jew's at it again!, they add, typical! He crawls from under the ruins, rummages out what he stashed, flogs it, gorges himself and gets fat, he sits in the coffee house and does crooked deals. He's a profiteer, a black marketer, a turkey cock. He dresses up and talks from his high horse. Until someone knocks him off, and someone will soon, people say, people are making threats, talking menacingly, I hear it on every street corner.

Meanwhile the paper puts out news, Irén carries on writing, that the mill is overcharging for grinding, they're tampering with the flour, to pull a fast one over on the workers, and so the article's author demands they be handled with extreme severity. And the next day in the same place it's revealed the police have arrested the cheating mill owner, Rejtő, with his employee, Jungreisz, otherwise his nephew. And now against these two men there was a protest of ironworkers who flooded in from Diósgyőr, filled the street, and shouted: Protect the new money! Jew-speculators, breaking our forint! Dirty Jews!

And I don't believe my eyes, carries on Irén, when in front of St Anne's Church, at the junction in the tramlines, they block the way of the tram, because someone must have recognized the very two public enemies riding past at that moment. Despite the police escort, they tear the two off the tram and shove the two Jewish mill owners in our direction, in front of the crowd. Supposedly the lone policeman just happens to be escorting them to labour, exactly at this hour, along this route—but who could believe such a coincidence?

The rabble is standing in front of them: Who do we have here? Rejtő and Jungreisz? And are you not happy to see us? Is that how your people bid someone good day? So tell me little birdies how'd you earn yourself the royal escort?

The terrified men taken prisoner could say anything or nothing at all, either way they will only work up the lynchers even more. Who, in a rage, grab the two and drag them away. They hang signs around their necks: Death to the forint-killers!—even though the forint was only verging on being launched. On the other they paint: I profited from pork meat price-gouging—hang me up!

We watch on from the other side, rooted to the spot with fear, horrified, and see as they beat them, writes Irén, and trail both along the street tied to a chain. First past the city hall, where some sort of gathering has started, there they show them like bears at the market, and then someone has the idea that the petrol station is the place to string up the ropes.

At the petrol station, the men end up in the grips of young lads, striplings really, and shrieking, incensed women who pull the rucksacks from the men's shoulders and open them, producing—but of course—such rarities as salami, chocolate, sardines or coffee. The types of things these proletarian mothers and sons haven't seen in years. The prisoners vainly defend themselves, that the food's not theirs, they were brought from the jail, they only got a daily allotment—it makes no difference, the people start beating the men. Grabbing Sándor Rejtő by the chain looped around his neck, they drag him along the ground, Ernő Jungreisz begs for his uncle's life, who at the last minute is saved by a squad of policemen led by a lieutenant colonel.

But the crowd turns on the police: You're not taking the Jews anywhere, there's no way in hell! And that nobody need dare try to shut them up, of course they're talking back, that's right, the workers of Miskolc talk back, got it? At which the police get scared, say OK then, in that case they'll not take the hostages to the hospital, instead whoever wants can drive them around town on the back of this lorry and show the people what happens to anybody who runs up prices. And who's a Jew, someone adds.

Eventually, the police lift only Rejtő, beaten within an inch of his life, onto the back of the lorry, while carelessly leaving Jungreisz behind, and so for want of anything better, the steadily surging rage of the lynchers turns on the nephew.

I believe in Kunvadas you witnessed something similar, Mária, interjects Irén, which is why I'm telling you this.

They throw a rope around the young man's neck and tie him to the back of a dray, to make him run behind it, but he's no longer able. He faints, the cart trails him along the ground on his back, his head knocks on the cobbles, his face turns blue, his neck stretches, and still they don't stop beating him.

*

Horror seeped through me as I reread Irén Hámos' words, but I couldn't tear my mind from them. Terrified, I began thinking how much this would damage our appeal; whether they wouldn't, as a result of the fresh pogrom, now want to make an even greater example.

I couldn't gather the strength to go over to my father's and discuss this latest development, so I locked myself in again and pretended as though nobody was home.

It was maybe about three in the afternoon when I realized I was starving. I'm losing my mind, I say, at the same hour a day ago in Keleti Train Station in Budapest I would have gladly eaten a stale bread roll but had nothing, and there wasn't a bite to eat in the house either. In the pantry I found a couple of last year's potatoes and an onion starting to rot, plus a rancid hunk of fatback—all right, I say, I'll make a potato soup. I break some dry twigs into the basket, throw a half-dozen corncobs and a log of false acacia on top, light the stove, and toss in the soup bits.

I'm about to ladle the soup into a bowl when I hear someone rapping at the gate. I don't care who it is, I'm not opening the door, I say. But they keep on knocking.

Eventually Irén Hámos appears in front of me—simply walks into my kitchen. She says she came in through the small garden gate that was off the latch, because she thought I might be at the back of the house somewhere and couldn't hear her knocking at the gate. She could see I was home, there was smoke coming out the chimney.

As we ate the soup, I told her I had read her letter, and Irén said she came to Kunvadas with her son, and because of the situation in Miskolc they're going to stay a while at Grandma's, it'll be safer that

183

way. Huh, I think, who would have thought so back in May? It turned out her husband sent them off immediately on the Friday early-morning train. Because he was panicking, but hopefully over nothing.

Panicking about what?, I asked.

He was scared the lynchers would attack our house.

I didn't understand why they would attack her house, because although I did read about those atrocities in her letter, I didn't believe that the Hámoses could get into trouble just because they were half Jewish, because who knew in Miskolc anyway.

It's not just that.

It's not?

From what she told me next, it became clear there was indeed reason for Irén to be worried for her husband, but Hámos wasn't willing to come back with them. Or if he wanted to, he didn't dare risk disobeying orders and deserting. But the worry was killing Irén, she could see how I must have felt in my own situation. At first of course I hadn't a clue why she was speaking this way and then bit by bit I understood. Though only later did the true crux of the matter reveal itself.

I learnt, for example, what Irén was able to prise out of her husband only the night before leaving, that's to say, the first live ammunition Hámos was entrusted with in his new position; he and some others were required to make preparations for General Secretary Mátyás Rákosi's rally in Miskolc, scheduled for 23rd July. Not only did this entail that as large a crowd as possible must attend, since during working hours the activists of the Diosgyőr ironworks and other nearby factories could easily mobilize the otherwise disgruntled workers in significant numbers, but, via the cadres, the workers must also be made to understand that the rally would address bringing an end to inflation and the replacement of the devalued pengő, and therefore—according to the party's own phrasing—the necessary foundations for economic stabilization. The workers must sound their dissatisfaction as loudly as possible and demand order be brought, explained Irén, so the Communist Party could head up these initiatives and declare what was to be done. On the one hand, uncompromisingly exposing the people thwarting stabilization and their methods—that's to say, the black-marketeering reactionaries who must be stopped in their conspiracies by all means—on the other, launching the forint, that was financially ready for introduction.

At the rally, the party leader spoke with fervour about these goals. Many afterwards jovially recounted how Comrade Rákosi—as usual—hadn't minced his words, how during one colourful turn of phrase he made explicit threats against the enemies of the working people: the speculators. Nationwide we have heard the same, he says, that though the new currency is barely yet born, already there are those who speculate against it. But our opinion is: any person who speculates with the forint, who intends to undermine the economic foundations of our democracy, must hang from the gallows.

This threat left Irén, who attended the rally, truly speechless. Particularly because it was met with a frightening murmur of agreement. And the same fear coursed into her a week later as pure terror at the lynching by the petrol station, when she was handed one of the thousands of distributed leaflets, because on it, the same bloodthirsty threat from the same speech was reproduced in the form of direct incitement.

At home she immediately had an argument with Ferrie, because sadly it very much looked like this reprinted incitement had indeed reached its target, people were almost literally torn to pieces. How could he say otherwise, both of them having witnessed what happened?

Red in the face, her husband could only stammer, while she carried on telling him that, before the attack, the reporters had focused on the same incitement. The papers had relentlessly protested that the profiteering mill owner was still a free man, though there wasn't a man in the whole city better fit for the noose than Mr Rejtő, who wasn't willing to sell flour to the Communist Party's own printing press at a lawful rate but at twice the price—abiding by the ancient teachings of his community. Of course, we know who conspire to run up prices, except now these reactionary exploiters operate by class rather than by race.

Answer me this, Irén put a question to her husband, how could it be possible that while there was no trial to establish what crime these two unfortunate wretches might have committed, the newspaper was already discussing, as though fact, that they had been making illicit profits from the workers' flour, and that the racketeers' collusions had been exposed? And the day after the lynching, the story that appeared in the paper put it as though the rightfully outraged crowd had known for certain that these two black marketeers had inflicted grave financial damage on the city's population and infringed the government's stabilization orders, and as though responding irately to this crime, the crowd attacked the men on the tram. And the article's title indicated that a popular verdict was delivered in Miskolc.

Listen, Ferrie, I say, what do we call a popular verdict? Because I think it's a lynching we want to present as lawful—though obviously such a thing is illogical. Well, Ferrie just hums and haws and says nothing. But nobody can tell me that those happenings had nothing to do with what was published in the newspaper the day before! How does an article like this get printed, I tell him, that urged these people be hanged from the gallows for trading illegally?

And Ferrie replies that the article urged nothing, it just pointed out the reactionaries' responsibility, and that illegal trading is damaging and therefore mustn't be tolerated.

Uh-huh, and the leaflet?, I say, Which literally threatened them with the gallows?

But Irén had cornered her husband in vain, she didn't get any answer, they made practically no progress, and, besides, Ferrie had to rush back to the party office. It was only afterwards, on the Thursday night, before she took the train, she managed to coax any sort of admission out of him. That their task in the party was to stoke the workers' dissatisfaction, and indeed his boss dictated this particular leaflet to Ferrie, who personally handled its printing and distributed it to the relevant places.

I swear, Mária, dearest, said Irén through tears, wringing her hands, I had no idea about any of it. That I needn't have looked far because it was none other than my own husband on that leaflet demanding the people be hanged. Sprinting to and fro with copy between the party office and the editorial office.

Irén, that's awful, I say, but I still don't understand why your husband need fear the lynchers that he had some part in inciting.

Well, of course, how could I understand, she's still only told me the first chapter of the Miskolc pogrom. She'll tell me in a second what happened next if I haven't heard already. But could we not sit out on the veranda? She would love to smell that rose bush.

As for the preceding events, continued Irén Hámos outside, turning her wicker chair to face the garden and sitting, by the time the police brought the Tuesday lynching to an end, and untied Ernő Jungreisz from the back of the horse and dray that trailed him along the cobbled road, the poor young man was dead. Later they counted more than a hundred puncture wounds and contusions around his body.

The arrests began the next day at dawn on Wednesday, 31st July—the police having spent the night at the station trying to gather from their moles and informers the names of the lynching's perpetrators and ringleaders. The same night her husband and his colleagues in the party argued about how the incident unfolded and how to judge it. After a talk with their superiors, their assessment of what happened on 30th July was that the ironworkers marched into Miskolc in an orderly formation, with the aim of—what else?—peacefully demonstrating their demand that the enemies of stabilization be punished, as is incidentally prescribed by order of the government. But when the two black marketeers were made to alight from the tram and escorted into town, the workers indeed began protesting against the two men but didn't voice any anti-Semitic epithets. Perhaps they didn't, Irén pursed her lips, but it was Jews they were cursing.

By that point, the organized workers had correctly sensed what their leaders expected of them. That with the strength of their own clearly stated action, they would be supporting the Communist policy—be it by looting the Smallholders' or Civic Party offices, or flushing idle reactionaries out of the coffee houses and rounding them up. Moreover, they had clear instruction not to hold back while expressing their righteous proletarian anger, especially with Jews caught red-handed, in case it somehow got out that the Communist Party was the Jews' party. Thus Ferrie and his colleagues were duly briefed to make sure everything was clear: the masses who attacked the two profiteering mill owners didn't end up in these confused circumstances at their own fault, hence, the ironworkers must not be branded as fascists, which would be hugely detrimental for our party. Therefore, the papers were to spread a few articles about the villainous duo's dirty past to make it clear why they had to be assailed.

Another important morsel from this night-time debriefing was that the Communist Party county secretary had—together with the leaders of the Social Democrats—tried to save the two black marketeers from the mass despair, as it were, but unfortunately to no avail. Irén, however, didn't see or hear anything of the sort, though she was there until the end.

While she told me all this, she took a liking to the phrase 'a popular verdict resulting from mass despair', repeating it a few times, as she stood up, and went to the kitchen to pour herself a glass of water.

*

I'm afraid I can't offer you a second course, I said apologetically to Mrs Hámos, but she wouldn't hear of me going to any trouble for her. What's more, on the shelf she found the ersatz tea that my Sándor often made for himself, and which I didn't dare to offer to anyone, but Irén said she likes it, she often drinks it herself. So I stoked the embers and put on the kettle.

I was thinking how this story was just pouring from her without me so much as asking a question, when she started again.

So, are you interested in hearing the rest of the Miskolc pogrom, Mária, dear?

Of course, only . . . I thought we could wait for the water to boil, and in the meantime . . .

In the meantime?, she asked, and looked at me inquiringly.

Good God! I almost said out loud, Is it so bizarre to expect a single measly question, a speck of interest in the opposite direction? Can it only ever be what she's been through that interests us?

It's just I came back last night too, I stammered, and I'm still . . .

Well, finally it crosses her mind that my own husband was sentenced to death a couple of days prior. Her hand goes to her mouth, Oh, of course, because . . . !, she yelps.

But then, though she asked, I didn't go into any detail, at which for want of anything better she reiterated the same empty assurances she had written to me. Now I was sorry I pushed her, because what could one say about a thing like that anyway. And then she acted oddly when I mentioned gratefully the comforting words in her letter—she became confused, asking when she wrote, and in what regard? Oh, because it was the day before the lynching . . . !

Once I had returned her to her story, she began by saying, that on 31st July in the morning, a couple dozen street hooligans were taken into police custody. According to the officially published news, a few factory workers indeed ended up among them but were immediately released upon being questioned. Sixteen or seventeen people remained behind bars whose interrogation was started by the police's deputy political commissar, a certain First Lieutenant Fogarasi. Who, it couldn't be ignored after all that had happened, was himself of Jewish descent—Irén even discovered that his father was a well-known vinegar and alcohol distiller who was killed along with his family in '44.

He made no effort to hide this under his cap, in fact supposedly he commenced the interrogation by lining up the company and telling them: It's not of your concern but I'll tell you nevertheless, I am First Lieutenant Artúr Fogarasi—in my previous position, I was the son of Frenkl, the liquor distiller.

Both inside the police jail and outside on the street the people whispered behind his back, What did he say? Whose son? But there was always someone who knew, the Miskolc distiller's son, Frenkl's son. And is the old man alive? Of course not, the only one left of the whole clan is this Artúr here, who took up a post at the station as the political investigator.

According to Irén—at least this was what she had heard—we were to picture him marching up and down the line of detainees, spitting into their faces: The lynchers—namely, yourselves—will confess to everything. Anyone who denies will be beaten by my men. Am I being understood?

But supposedly the appointed investigators only beat two of the suspects who denied they took part in the lynching—and

Fogarasi had not personally contributed to any violent inter-rogation. Yet when some were released, apparently they started exaggerating, spreading word that torture was being used, and in the blink of an eye throngs of furious people were on the street. So furious, they straight away attacked another Jew on the market square—forming a circle, shouting and shoving, when a detective dispersed the mob with a warning shot.

Many spread the word that it was also thanks to the efforts of the Communist organizers that the number attending the following day's rally, on 1st August, had surged to ten thousand. They heard that workers had arrived not only from nearby Ózd, Sajószentpéter and Kazincbarcika, but also on charter trains across the country from Csepel, Győr and Szombathely. Many believed that this mass anger was fuelled by the Communists to help others recognize that the only way to bring about order was through the nationalization of the major factories.

Yet this political rally, which had started earlier, was practically swept away by the other, unconnected, spontaneous mass demon-stration—or was it already a violent revolt?—which set out demanding the release of the perpetrators of the previous day's lynching. Irén doesn't know whether Ferrie was making calls from the party office to Csepel, for example, inviting the organized workers to Miskolc to participate in the rally, or whether he was focused on the organization and reinforcement of a cordon, tasked to hold back the crowds. No matter how it happened, it looked like the Communists themselves had let the genie out of the bottle, which was now turning against them. More precisely against their own police, because the Ministry of the Interior, led by László Rajk, was under the Communists.

If the party leaders had truly tried to defend the two mill owners, now they were bracing themselves for action a second time—Irén believed her husband must have assumed an active role in the defensive efforts. The stewards supervising the rally formed a cordon by linking arms, while in front of the line of defence were positioned loud agitators, on account of their highly persuasive abilities to bring the crowd to its senses and to stop it laying siege. However, not only did the crowd disperse them within minutes, it gave many of them chase too—some following stewards the whole way home and beating them up in their own house. Poor Ferrie received his fair share of punches too, one of the Diosgyőr workers even recognized him, shouted his name and taunted him, that there was no use in running, they would find him, because now every last Jew-commie traitor to the workers was going to be strung up.

Irén Hámos poured herself a cup of tea and sat out on the veranda again, where the dusk was now glowing dark red between the trees in the garden. She looked out and continued, how utterly terrified her husband was when he made it home on Thursday night.

First Lieutenant Fogarasi has been beaten to death by the fascist mob, said Hámos to his wife, meanwhile sweating and shaking profusely.

Bit by bit, Irén managed to coax from her husband where he had been, what he had witnessed and what he himself had done. First Hámos talked about how the left-wing parties' stewards initially tried to establish a cordon, blocking the oncoming tide of people, which surged unstoppably towards its destination—none other than the police station. But they were broken up by the crowd just as they

193

realized how menacing the situation was, after all, the crowd meant to lay siege to an edifice under the protection of armed policemen.

And that's when Ferrie and his colleagues received the order from their superiors, that if the human cordon hasn't been successful, they were to carry on their resistance efforts but individually while maintaining contact with one another, and by no means are they to leave their positions because that would qualify as desertion. They were to carry on preventing the crowd from mounting an attack against the police station.

Hámos told his wife the details of their bold efforts, when he himself and one of his colleagues had openly stood before the tumult to bring it to a stop—using the simplest of means. Turning to face it, they held out their arms and said, Stop, stop, everyone stop.

Friends!, said Ferrie, raising a hand purposefully, this is the endpoint of our march and we ask your patience as we wait for the others to arrive. There will be an official appeal, followed by an announcement, explained Ferrie to the surprised demonstrators, after which we ask you to peacefully, quietly . . .

And he got no further, drowned out by invectives: Who are you lot? What do you want?

Well, we're organizers, he says, on behalf of the Social Democrats and the Communists . . .

You're not organizing this one, pal! This here's a working-class protest, for the real workers!

Even so, we should all respect peace and order . . .

What do you want to respect? The jeers were peppered with filthy language: Where do you see a whiff of peace here? Or patience? When there's only hunger and prison. We've come to free our leaders, we have to stop the torture interrogations, repeated the people—that's when Ferrie and his colleague decided it would be best to split and make themselves scarce.

Nevertheless, continued Irén, her husband stayed on the scene so on the one hand he could be a witness to whatever happened in the front lines of the siege, where the most hostile gangs were gathered, and on the other he could get shreds of news from inside the station by catching hold of one or two familiar detectives or typists who had sneaked out the back door.

He learnt that inside the station, utter chaos had broken out when they saw this crowd that was bigger yet than Tuesday's. In all probability, Fogarasi's superiors left the first lieutenant to fend for himself, nor did he know who was protesting and why. He was of the understanding that the worker crowds were still protesting against the running up of prices and black marketeers, and supposedly he was speculating how to make them understand not to raise a storm because the police were in agreement with them. So he was indeed surprised when informed that, though there were of course chants similar to those in the previous days, such as, a full day of work, nothing on the plate and hang the profiteers, traitors to the workers; it was all engulfed by their demand for the immediate release of the detainees. No more Jews brutalizing workers.

Outside the station, meanwhile, the lord lieutenant appeared with a Russian soldier escort and began giving a speech. He urged everyone to remain calm and promised that if they drew back, their representatives would be heard out, but hardly anything he said was audible over the people's booing and jeering at the Russians. And when the Soviet city commandant spoke, with the aid of an interpreter, the booing grew louder and many openly mocked him.

The crowd turned again towards the windows of the police station, chanting and calling: Fogarasi, free the prisoners! Fogarasi, stop the torture! We'll not stand by, as the Jew-police torture our worker leaders to death! And once again: Fogarasi, free the prisoners!

The first lieutenant was said to be genuinely surprised that the crowd were referring to the detained lynchers as the leaders of the workers' demonstration. He was astounded by the change in atmosphere. None of them are demanding better provisions?, he asked his men.

We don't know, sir, but it makes no difference now. The point is they're about to lay siege on us. We asked for assistance from the Soviet city commandant but they declined. We only have one option: We have to release those prisoners!

And so, fruitlessly, the first lieutenant tried to convince his subordinates not to let Jungreisz's murderers go, after their own tireless work in picking the lynchers up. Everyone besides Fogarasi said it was better to let these bastards cut and run, to settle the crowd.

Yet when they opened the locks and shoved out the bandits, not only did tempers not cool but in fact they hit a second wave. Especially because the besiegers noticed, in one fell swoop, the number of policemen and detectives escaping in civvies and so could begin calculating how few were left inside.

The lieutenant looked out on the square and suddenly saw only one valid option. The crowd's besieging force demanded immediate action.

Line up at the windows!, he ordered. Firing positions!

Firing positions . . . ?, the deputy cocked his head to one side. With fifteen men, sir? Against tens of thousands? Who'll stand guard over the prisoners? Many have taken off . . . Our men will never dare to open fire!

They won't?

They're scared the crowd will tear them limb from limb! Sir, excuse me for speaking out of line, but . . . at this point, resistance against such superior numbers makes no sense.

They'll kick your head in the second you step out the door!, said one policeman to another.

Downstairs, the besieging crowd began smashing the windows and setting upon the gate with crowbars. At which Fogarasi gave the order to open fire, but only a few obeyed with tentative shots from one or two of the upper windows.

Someone entered the room and shouted: They've broken down the door! They're coming up the stairs!

From then on, all that could be heard were the voices of the attackers. The heated calls and unfinished half-sentences of the hunt, and the cheers as they found Fogarasi. We've got the bastard! Where is he? He was hiding in the coal cellar! There were attackers who didn't know who he was—he's the detective, the one torturing the prisoners. The pálinka distiller's fella? That's right! Give him one then!

*

Thinking back, after that story, I truly don't understand how Irén and I could listen to the entirety of the Prime Minister's radio speech. Irén stood up, said the speech was starting soon and she wanted to get home because she couldn't miss it. Unless I turned it on and we listened together. But why didn't I protest?

Oh, he's talking to us, all right, laughed my guest, when Mátyás Rákosi first thanked the farmers' wives, who had borne the lion's share of the burden of inflation. The shocking suffering hadn't broken the people's faith in democracy, and the reactionary's attempts had been shipwrecked on the self-assurance and the maturity of our industrious people.

All the graver and more damnable is the aberration, he raised his voice, which happened on the threshold of economic rehabilitation in Miskolc. It has revealed that the renascent reactionaries and the fascism that lurks behind them will not shy from provocation if, by such methods, they can do damage to our young democracy—now, of all times, when the success of economic rehabilitation will pull out from under its feet the soil of inflation, from which sprouts the bulk of workers' dissatisfaction, added Rákosi with greater vigour. He believes what occurred in Miskolc, however, was a serious attempt to upset economic rehabilitation, every Miskolc worker must understand this. Just watch the reactionaries gloat, and immediately any worker will see he made a grave mistake when he succumbed to such excesses, and to cap it all, came to the defence of criminals waiting to be brought to account by the law.

We understand the desperation that fuelled the exploited, impoverished workers of Miskolc, said Rákosi, switching to a more sanctimonious vernacular, and we understand the anger against speculators and black marketeers. But most vigorously of all, we condemn the form and the manner, he raised his voice, in which it manifested. Such excesses inflict grave damage upon the country, and are the wishes of the very people who are enemies to the economic recovery of our democracy. He is certain the majority of the Miskolc workers know this, and will no longer give way to newer provocations in any form. But will help bring before the law and punish those who, out of blind fervour or cold reactionary calculation, on the eve of economic rehabilitation, so tarnish our good news.

Finally, he brought up the forint defence associations that were formed across the country and in places overzealously set up gallows for the enemies of the forint. And as though forgetting that only recently he himself had demanded exactly this, in Miskolc, he now forbade any such thing because it did more damage than good. He then reassured the radio listeners that the government had issued tough rulings that, if necessary, would sentence death by the rope to any person attempting to undermine the fledgling forint.

I needn't explain the mood that overcame me after he permitted himself once again to threaten the rope, but I thought it best to say nothing. Once I switched off the radio, however, Irén too thought with horror that somebody would be called to task.

When she worries about her husband, she said, indeed it's their own people she fears most. After all, what happened in Miskolc was a repeat of Kunvadas: the monstrous crowd tore living people to pieces, and so without question there would be an investigation into who was responsible. And the investigators would immediately assume the lyncher's anger was stoked when the deadly threat from the rally speech was hammered into the public. So, that's what they have to cover up and extricate themselves from, to save their own skin. She feared that if the Communists were forced to wash their hands of this matter, not only would they stand Ferrie before a disciplinary committee, he would take the fall for criminal liability—or he alongside others. And so they would place her husband on trial as an inciter, just as they did my own. Indeed, due to the articles and leaflets, unfortunately, Ferrie's genuine role in the whipping up of the murderous climate really would be unmistakable—however indirect and unintentional.

She is alone with this frenzy of nervous thoughts, of course, she and her husband haven't spoken a word about it. On Friday morning, at dawn, when Ferrie escorted her to the train station, though still terrified of a lynching, he said some words of comfort, that Irén wasn't to fret, last night the Minister of the Interior personally set about restoring order and would stay in the city for as long as it took. In the morning, all the shops would open which had been closed since Tuesday and the day would start in the factories with August's wages. And because the wages would be in forint, for the first time, the Communists had to be there too, so they could celebrate the new money with the workers.

Later on, chatting over fresh cups of tea, imagining who could be such beasts that in their droves wouldn't flinch at tearing even living people to pieces, our conversation turned to Etel Radai. Apparently, before the war, Irén worked as an assistant nurse for a doctor in Karcag, and during her time there, met a rather primitive but mawkishly chatty young woman, Etel, who wanted to be a nurse whatever it took, but of course everyone sent her away. Around that time, the same Etel whispered to Irén, in confidence, that her lover forced her to have a termination and then ran off with another woman. And now she can never have children, a doctor told her so, not the one who performed the curettage. That's why she wants to help sick children, so why will nobody let her?

But do I know what she really doesn't understand?, asked Irén then. What that Gergely Kátai had wanted when he ordered us out of Kunvadas. Does he have a personal grievance with Ferrie? Or else what could be behind it? I must know something because she heard that he's best friends with my husband.

I honestly don't know, I haven't the faintest idea, I replied. The truth is it wasn't Gergely who was Sándor's best friend, but rather his late wife, Anna, was my best friend, who died giving birth. Actually—under fairly suspicious circumstances—in Etel Radai's presence. And Sándor was landed with my Anna's husband as an addendum really—before then they had been distant acquaintances. And I think I wasn't the only one who understood Kátai less and less, my husband would say the same now.

As Irén was about to leave—we were standing in the garden— something else crossed her mind, maybe I could give her an answer. That during the lynching here, supposedly it was one of the Rosenstein boys who was killed at the airstrip. What have I heard? Was this true? And which one was it? And what news do I have of the Rosenstein brothers in general?

To which I told her quite briefly that of the three, József the soda-water man, the youngest, was the only one to survive the war, and yes, sadly it was he who died on the day of the pogrom at the airstrip.

So not poor Ernő then . . . For a long time I imagined it was Ernő who survived the war, said Irén, tilting her head pensively. And then she told me that she knew Ernő Rónai, the architect, through her relatives in Karcag, they kept the same company. There were dances and summer jaunts where they used to meet and Ernő would be there too—Irén talked as if my story with Ernő had left her mind completely, though perhaps she really didn't remember me—and now, she has to confess, she said, everyone was in love with Ernő.

With that, she took her leave and left me here with such memories and desires resurrected from the distant past. Full of thought, I collapsed into the wicker chair and reclined—as the waltzing male figure I remembered from the carnival ball pulled me close, though he wore only a leather apron and strangely I wasn't repulsed by the smell of his sweat. Nor, more unusually, by my own desire, which I now suddenly felt, pulling my feet up onto the seat of the chair.

Later, it occurred to me that finally Irén Hámos had again managed to forget about my husband and hadn't shared my faith that Sándor could avoid the harshest of sentences. As she had left, she sighed about what the situation might be in Miskolc, and whether the hooligans had attacked her husband too.

*

For a long spell afterwards, I stopped making notes. When the life of one's husband is hanging by a thread, what's there to jot in a diary? Every passing day the same dread, the same hopeful prayer? But then at last, I could pick up the pen again.

I couldn't believe it. At the hearing of the appeal that had followed the Budapest trial, a decision was finally reached and Sándor was acquitted.

In that instant, such a weight lifted from my heart, I couldn't even bear to move. Yet another thing to recover from, I suddenly thought.

This court of the second instance deviated from the first judgement in every way. It found different people guilty for different reasons, didn't judge the accused's actions the same way, and didn't impose the same penalties.

The crucial information published in the papers was that schoolmaster Sándor Hadnagy had been acquitted in the absence of a criminal offence, Smallholders Secretary Gergely Kátai received two and a half years instead of the rope, while Zsigmond Rácz's death sentence as inciter was changed to a life sentence. The rest of the accused's prison sentences were softened from eight years to as short as five months.

For my husband's case, this day finally delivered complete justice—but I didn't want to opine on the sentences given to the rest. Best to say nothing, I thought, and felt desperately tired.

The instant the sentence was announced publicly, Sándor had yet to leave his condemned cell and the streets were already swarming with shrieking hawkers, the *Fresh News* was out. Leftists furious about soft sentencing in Kunvadas pogrom trial! Leftists demand another hearing! What treatment awaits the perpetrators of the Miskolc lynching?, blared the criers.

*

Irén Hámos welcomed the news of my husband's acquittal in a new letter on the same day—I was leaving for the station to await Sándor's release in Budapest when the postman handed me an envelope. So I opened Irén's letter on the train, which read, she of all people can understand, I must be immensely relieved that the earlier death sentence has been exchanged for a ruling of total innocence and his immediate release. Honestly speaking, I couldn't tell whether Irén didn't mean to mix a hint of sarcasm into her words because she may deem my husband to be guilty still on certain accounts. It was odd in any case that in the same letter she found space for further details of the Miskolc police officer's lynching— which, thanks to the more thorough newspaper articles, I could picture already.

Because through her husband, Irén got her hands on some kind of interrogation reports, or extracts from which certain confessions had been copied and passed from one hand to the next. In them, the defendants stated that when they started to beat First Lieutenant Fogarasi with pick handles and iron pipes, among them were not only men but women, youngsters and children too. When asked whether the crowd at the police station only wanted to square matters with the Jewish interrogators, most replied that they wanted to catch the non-Jews too but couldn't find them. Several went on to say they sunk a miner's pick into Fogarasi's shoulder and, when a dray pulled into the courtyard, used the same pick to pin the palm of his hand to the back. And then, in a frenzy, they trailed him in circles around the yard. He was unconscious by the time they carried him out to the street and threw him on the back of a lorry.

Passers-by asked who it was, where they were taking him, and upon learning it was Artúr Fogarasi, the Jewish officer, the torturer,

Frenkl's son, and that he was going to be hanged, with a shower of bloodthirsty calls the pedestrians ran after the lorry. Which got a puncture and couldn't go on.

Get that Jew down, he can walk like the rest of us!, they shouted, but upon trying to stand him on his feet, said, this lad's not going to hoof it.

Well, he can crawl! Ring a rope around his neck! But that won't work either, said another, he'll be strangled right away. Then around his feet, pull him by his feet instead.

And so they started trailing the body along the road towards the market square, meanwhile, whoever could squeeze close spat at, booted and beat it. Eventually, a teenage boy ran over and started hitting it with a hammer.

*

Seeing my husband for the first time outside the prison's rear entrance?—I don't know what to write. I was happy and relieved but somehow struck with such paralysis that I spent the whole day sluggishly doubting whether I could even stay awake. After he had smoked his first cigarette on a bench, I asked Sándor, does he not want to spend a couple of days more in Budapest? But he wouldn't hear a word of it, let's get out of here before they change their minds.

Back at my accommodation—before packing my things—we still left ourselves enough time for Sándor to put his arms around me. After I unfolded the lavender from his handkerchief to press my face into it, he gently tipped me onto my back and whispered to let the pleasure overpower me. I didn't understand what he meant but when he insisted I shouldn't be so terrified of love, bravely, clenching my teeth, I endured and finally managed not to pull away from under him.

On the train, I talked at length about Irén Hámos' visit and letters, about the Miskolc pogrom and that, actually, when times were hard, Irén was the only person who spared a thought and spoke to me with any compassion.

I also told my husband and even showed him what Irén wrote about Minister of the Interior László Rajk. That at the news of the pogrom, Rajk came to Miskolc, where upon assembling the police force, he suspended the officers and kicked out half the staff as suspicious elements. Next, he published an announcement, which read that in Miskolc the disciplined worker's party march was pushed to fascistic-mannered provocation by pro–Arrow Cross elements, but investigations have confirmed that culpability rested with propaganda circulated by suspicious outsiders who infiltrated the city. In the last days, he says, during multiple police raids citywide, we have exposed the whereabouts of Arrow Cross and Western agents, have checked the papers of nearly four thousand people, and, in multiple houses, have uncovered and seized reactionary documents and caches of arms.

Meanwhile, they say the city mayor whispered into Rajk's ear: Mr Minister, sir, the Jews . . . !

Jews? What Jews?!

Well, the Israelite community. They would like to pay their respects to the lynched First Lieutenant Fogarasi with a religious burial.

Absolutely not! It would only provoke more anti-Semitic mania. He'll get a police officer's state funeral. With a three-volley salute, as is proper!

But Sándor just hummed and hawed in stony silence for the entire journey. When we arrived home, he started saying he didn't want to cause a scene on the train but to be perfectly honest, he doesn't like this friendship of mine with Mrs Hámos one bit. He believes her intentions were well-meaning and sympathetic and understands why this was of comfort at the time, but that the matter is over, there's no need anymore. Besides, Ferrie Hámos was always skulking around the leftists and the armed men, instead of looking for a proper job. So, obviously, he's state security now, in other words, we best hope we never hear of him again. And then Sándor made fouler remarks about both, though without any recent news about either, merely piling on more prejudices in his growing irritation because we were at loggerheads. But the last words before lying down were that's enough of that, let's never bring it up again.

*

Mrs Irén Hámos wrote her last letter to me in October '46—I remember it was around the time when we learnt that though Sándor was acquitted, he still couldn't go back to teaching, his college application was rejected, so I would have to become the breadwinner.

For a couple of sentences, Irén beat about the bush—she asked how we were and how Sándor held up against everything that happened—but then with a hint of shame she confessed her real intention. Because I must understand her husband's position, who fortunately didn't have to face trial, but his bosses certainly gave him a thorough dressing down and now the requirements he has to obey are stricter than ever. For example, he can never talk to anyone about the pogrom. But perhaps not just the Miskolc pogrom, the Kunvadas one too—at least, when she read him the news in the paper that Sándor Hadnagy had been acquitted, Ferrie crossly changed the subject straight away. And so she didn't want to annoy him more by telling him about our meetings and her letters to me, that's to say, she hasn't discussed it with him, but she believes the duty of confidentiality includes her too, as his wife. So she asks me, to please understand her and to promise, I won't tell anyone a word of what I heard from her. And I will send back her letters by return of post so she can destroy them—including the one I am reading.

By the by, as an afterword to the story, she wants me to know (but, if possible, I must read this too with closed eyes) that in the Miskolc-pogrom lawsuit, finally, thirty-five—mostly ironworkers and railway workers—ended up in the dock, of whom according to the news two were women and two were Gypsies. Yet, in comparison to the Kunvadas suit, this one followed vastly more up-to-date proceedings in two regards: firstly, in the charges there was no mention that the victims attacked were Jews and beaten to death as Jews, and, secondly, little by little, every last defendant was released.

By way of parting, again she asks that I please return her letters, that I forget everything, and wishing us well, closes for now, Irén.
